R I Vinnicombe is a bookseller living in Sefton, NSW, Australia.

Tales of Imagination and Mystery

R I Vinnicombe

First published by R I Vinnicombe in 2019
This edition published in 2019 by R I Vinnicombe

Tales of Imagination and Mystery

EPUB: 9780648696100
POD: 9780648696117

Cover design by Red Tally Studios

Publishing services provided by Critical Mass
www.critmassconsulting.com

Contents

THE GUIDE

The very neatly groomed and officious-looking girl at the desk said "Our guide is away to day. But you are quite welcome to walk through the house by yourself, in a self-guided tour. There are display boards in each room explaining everything. You'll find the house very interesting. And if you have any questions when you come out, I'll be pleased to answer them"

She was addressing Chris and Jenny who had walked up the long, winding drive, each holding a hand of their four year old son, Bobby, between them, to see The Old House, as it was rather unimaginatively called, because Jenny had noticed it as they were driving past, and she said it looked such an interesting old place, and the sign said "Guided Tours". Jenny was bright and bubbly, given to flights of impulse and was very superstitious. She wore charms and amulets and liked to wear long, flowing, mauve and pink and crimson dresses and scarves and sashes whenever she could. Anything old and interesting and spiritual and outre and off-beat fascinated her. Chris was much more pragmatic and thought "Seen one old house, you've seen them all." But he knew there was no stopping Jenny when she was set on doing something.

"Couldn't they have come up with a more imaginative name for this place than "The Old House" Chris asked the girl on the desk, who, according to a neat, gilt sign in front of her was called Carol, as if, because he was there under protest, he was looking for any reason to complain.

"Well, it's like this" said Carol.. The house never actually had a name. But after all the terrible things that happened here over 100 years ago, the owners decided to build a new house on the land, and abandon this one. So then you had the New House, and The Old House. But then the New House burned down, so all we are left with, unfortunately, is The Old House with all its awful memories".

"Maybe The Old House was jealous of The New House and caused it to burn down!" suggested Jenny, who loved attributing human characteristics to inanimate objects.

"Fire precautions were extremely crude in those days, and of course there were no fire brigades and there were many inflammable materials used in construction" explained Carol, in a coldly scientific tone.

"Do you know much about real history?" came back Jenny, as if she felt Carol was having a go at her.

Carol took off her glasses and waggled them in her fingers while she looked Jenny straight in the eye. She cleared her throat and said quietly but deliberately "I have an honours degree in history from Cambridge University…….". in a tone that implied "So there!"

"My wife also has a degree - of vivid imagination" said Chris, unable to resist the chance of making the quip. Then he added as he handed over the five dollars each for the two of them and walked towards the entrance. "Don't we get a discount for not having a guide?"

Then just as they were about to go in Carol stood up and walked towards them, looking at them keenly as if she had something important to impart.

"I'd better warn you there were multiple murders committed here 100 years ago. The then lady of the house, Evelyn Hardy, was what we would call now a paranoid schizophrenic, and she'd discipline her children unbelievably severely if they did anything wrong, - she'd burn their toys, or kill their pets in front of them, or make the boys dress as a girl and the girl dress as a boy, or even lock them in the cellar. And one day, she went totally off her rocker and killed her three children and then killed her husband,

George Hardy, when he tried to stop her. She threw the children off the roof and then because that didn't kill them, she ran downstairs and drowned them in the pond.

"And for that she was, by the way, hanged.

"I just thought I'd tell you so you'd be ready to be shocked when you read about it, because it's very dreadful and some people are understandably a bit queasy about it."

Jenny listened to it all with a mouth wide open in wonder, but when Carol had finished, exclaimed "Oooh! How exciting. I mean, it's awful, but how exciting!". She looked up at the old walls and the high ceiling. "Perhaps the spirits of these people are still inhabiting the house. I believe in that, you know. They say when people die prematurely their spirits linger on because they feel they were taken before their time ...."

Chris only rolled his eyes and commented "A schizo. Charming! Come on, let's get this over with."

But Jenny stood still, staring at the doorway they were about to enter, looking absolutely enervated and delighted at the prospect of what they might be going to see. She raised one hand towards the doorway with her palm facing forward.

"Come out! Come out spirits, wherever you are! Come out! We are friendly! We want to meet you! Don't be afraid! Come out"

Chris turned his face away pretending to look un-believably embarrassed.

"They'll think you've been on the spirits!" he said sarcastically.

The reception area of "The Old House" that they were in, where you paid your money and could pick up travel brochures and maps of the surrounding area or buy locally made wine or preserves was brightly lit and, though structurally a part of the house, had been decorated in a modern fashion. Now they walked into the original part of the house there was a sudden de-crease in light and it took a while for their eyes to become accustomed to the dimness. It felt as if they had really stepped back 100 years in time. They were in a large hallway from where doors led into other rooms and whose walls had large, sombre portraits of the family members who had once inhabited the house in elaborate, gilt frames, and mysterious landscapes of how the countryside once looked in its dim and distant past. The high ceiling of the hallway was ornate and there was an elaborate frieze all round. The wallpaper was richly brocaded dark pink with an off-white back-ground. There was imposing, polished furniture with elaborate carvings and a big glass display-cabinet with all sort of trinkets and bric a brac and household uten-sils of a style that would never more be seen.

There was a not unpleasant but distinct aroma of oldness in the air, but the practical Chris only looked up at the ceiling thinking what a pain it would be to have climb up to paint it, and get little brushes in and out of all those carvings. Jenny, however, ran her hand over the textured wallpaper in wonder. Then suddenly a soft female voice seemed to emanate from nowhere.

"Can I help you?"

Bobby, who had been holding his mother's hand, sucking his thumb and looking round with an expression of trepidation, gave out a yelp of surprise.

Chris and Jenny both turned and saw a short but amply built young woman in complete period costume, a dark blue floor-length dress, heavy black, laced shoes, lace cuffs and a lace collar, with dark, straight hair brushed back and tied in a bun behind, who had materialised out of the shadows. They had not seen anyone come in and had not seen anyone in the room when they entered it. Even now they could see her she seemed only just visible, and seemed to blend in with the rest of the hallway like another piece of the furniture.

"I am your guide for today" she added, in a soft, gentle voice as if she was overwhelmed with pleasure at being so. "I am so pleased you want to see the house". She had her hands clasped in front of her, and she was slightly round-shouldered, and her feet were somewhat apart with the toes tending outward.

Jenny beamed at her.

"Oh, what fun! But we were told you were away today:"

The guide, keeping the same posture, kept her eyes fixed on Jenny's face, showing no change of expression from the welcoming smile, except somehow looking as if she was debating an answer to Jenny's question within herself. Then finally she spoke.

"I have my own private entrance. I come and go as I please They often don't know if I'm here or not".

Jenny thought, well what was the point of that? if the girl on the outside desk didn't know if the guide was in or not, but said nothing. Then she looked the guide's costume up and down..

"Well, you certainly look the part. That dress looks like it was made for you. It's obviously very old, made to fit someone now long gone 100 years ago. How wonderful that it should be exactly your size"

The guide looked down at herself and frowned as if she didn't see the point of the remark, then raised her head and smiled. She stroked the front of the skirt fondly. "This is my day dress. I love it".

"But how come it fits you so exactly? It follows your shape like a glove."

The guide looked down at herself again. "I go in and out in all the wrong places, don't I? But I'm sorry to say that's the way it is after you've borne three children."

While she spoke she made a peculiar scratching motion at one side just where the waist of the dress was.

"Have you been bitten by a mosquito, dear?" inquired Jenny.

"Fleas" the guide smiled at her, still scratching.

Jenny looked at Chris and Chris looked at Jenny, who was slightly taken aback.

The guide looked at her slyly. "All the best people have fleas! Don't you know?"

Then she turned on her heels saying "But come this way with me and I'll give you the tour"

"Have you come a long way?" she asked them, looking back, as they followed her through a doorway.

"We've been driving for four hours" said Jenny.

"So the horses must be tired" said the guide with a sly smile.

Chris and Jenny looked at each other and frowned, but said nothing.

When the guide walked she kept her hands clasped in front of her. Because they couldn't see her legs under the long skirt, just the laced shoes, and because of her peculiar flat gait she seemed to float more than walk over the floor.

"Follow me. We are coming out of the grand entrance hall, going into the grand dining room. I always show guests the grand dining room first. I love it so much. Keep close to me, by the way, when I move from room to room, and don't be too distracted by anything you see, because this is somewhat of a rabbit-warren of a house. The rooms are joined to each other by confusing hallways that go in all sort of directions, with adjuncts and staircases and extra levels that were added over the years. But I love it! This house is my life. It is part of me, and I am part of the house"

She gave them a kind smile. "And I wouldn't want you to get lost! You might never be found again!"

Chris and Jenny looked at each other quite bemused, but kept following her.

As she walked across the dining room she put her hand inside her collar and ran it round to pull it away from her neck as if it was too tight. Then she ran her left hand round her right wrist, and her right hand round her left wrist, as if they were hurting her.

"What's the matter, dear?" asked Jenny when the guide stopped. "Is your collar too tight?"

Then, never being backward in coming forward, before the guide could answer she took the collar between her hands and waggled it to see how tight it was, to the guide's slight consternation.

"No it's not tight at all!" Jenny exclaimed.

The guide ignored the remark and suddenly looked very sullen and moved her own hand round inside the collar again.

"It's just….it's just ….I feel like….. my neck….is being squeezed …..sometimes…it feels there's something tight around it….and my wrists feel as if they've got something tight around them …..."

Then, just as suddenly, she snapped out of it, and the smile returned to her face and she clasped her hands before her again, but then quickly unclasped them to indicate the room.

"Here we are in the grand dining room. As you can see this marvellous table was made for great feasts - it can seat up to 22 people when the leaves are full extended. The central part is cut from one complete piece of cedar. Sometimes the table would be opened out to accommodate all the social hierarchy of the colony, when all the gossip and scandals and tales and secrets would be bouncing ground the walls of the room. Oh, wouldn't a historian have loved to be there with his notebook! Sometimes it would just be a small, intimate family gathering with cousins and sisters and uncles and close friends. As you can imagine when it was full complement of 22 guests, three maidservants and two cooks would be kept busy all evening preparing the food and running in and out to serve them".

Jenny took her camera out of her handbag. "Can we take pictures?" she asked gleefully.

The guide frowned and looked as if she didn't know what the Jenny was talking about. "Take….. pictures?.........No, the pictures must stay here. You can't take them. They belong to the house. What on earth makes you think you can just take them?"

"No. No. Photographs. with our camera!" She held the camera towards the guide, and the guide looked at it in horror as if it was a dangerous weapon and she had never seen such a thing before. "I have never seen a camera like that!" she muttered, as if totally confused

But before the guide had time to say anything more Jenny stepped back and clicked a picture of the dining table with the guide standing in front of it. The guide was caught with a look of utter surprise on her face, and at the flash she jumped and let out a little scream. Then Jenny turned the camera to show her the picture on the screen. The guide stared at it in astonishment, looked up at Jenny's face, then back at the screen. Then she frowned, looked at the floor, looked left and right, before a sly look come onto her face, she looked past them, and muttered to herself "Of course... the cameras are different now" then blinked, and was back in this world.

For some reason Bobby had been staring up at her with fear in his eyes since they had walked into the entrance hallway Suddenly on a whim the guide bent down and picked him up, and held him up high, much to the boy's distaste, and then hugged him to her.

"Oh, what a lovely little boy. I would love to have a little boy like this. Oh, he reminds me so much of my own poor little children when they were that age. It's such a lovely age. At this age they are little angels. It's only when they grow older they become little devils….."

However, despite her nice words Bobby recoiled as far as he could from her embrace, and was struggling to be put down. She appeared not to notice but hugged him to her for many seconds before she finally did let him down, to his evident great relief. He then retreated behind his mother and grabbed onto her dress, looking at the guide with fearful eyes.

"Are your children all grown up, then?" Jenny asked her.

The guide gave her a strange look, and for a second looked confused as if she didn't know how to answer. Then she looked past them and seemed to be debating within herself how to respond. Then she seemed to come to a conclusion and said dreamily, as if half to them and half to herself, "Oh……..I don't think they'll ever grow up…

"But come, I want you to see Evelyn's diary-room"

She led them out of the grand dining room into another hallway, and turned into a very small room with a small delicate lady's desk under a window, that had a window box full of flowers outside it. The afternoon sun was shining directly onto the desk where a big diary the size of a ledger lay open.

"This was Evelyn's little study" she said stopping at the desk "that she called her diary room, because it was where she would come to write her diary. She didn't just write it at just at night but anytime, just as the mood took her."

The diary was held open at one double page and fixed between glass in a frame so no-one could touch it. Jenny leaned down and tried to read the handwriting, but the ink was very faded, and the writing was erratic, uneven and troubled, and she could only make out a few words here and there.

But the guide stood over it, looked down on it lovingly, and started to read.

"Peace and quiet. George is away with the children. Oh how I love the silence. The peace. I could cut up big slices of the peace and store it away for when I have none...

"I will only admit to you, my diary, but the sound of my childrens' voices grates me. I had a dream last night, and it had an atmosphere of absolute joy. And when I woke up, for one house the feeling was still with me. Then the old terrors came again. I had the notion if I opened all the doors and all the shutters and let the wind blow though the house it would blow all the terrors away, so I did. but it made no difference, only some mosquitoes and blowflies blew in! So I closed them all again. Then I rearranged "at this point the guide looked up from the letter and into the distance, but she kept talking as if she knew he words by heart" ...all the furniture, the pieces I could lift anyway, so they all faced north west, back toward the old country, . . I have heard if all your furniture faces one way, you will one day go that way. Them the notion came upon me that one of the children had not gone with George, and was hiding in the house somewhere, watching me. So I looked in every room, behind every curtain, under every bed, up every chimney, down in the cellar, in every cupboard, but they were not there..."

"One good thing about them being away is I don't have to watch for them slipping poison into my food. I know they are trying to poison me. When I am away I can eat with such freedom. Neither do I have to wear my gloves, as I wipe clean everything they might have touched...."

Chris looked at her with an expression of uncomprehension, but Jenny was so impressed with her knowing the diary by heart she seemed to disregard the meaning of the words.

"You must have read that so many times you know it word for word" she interrupted the guide.

The guide went silent, and gazed out the window dreamily. "Yes......I must just remember it.." she muttered.

Jenny looked as though she was enchanted, but Chris's only comment was "So she was a total fruit loop, eh?"

At this the guide frowned and suddenly looked totally nonplussed, as if that wasn't the comment she was expecting. She looked down, left and right, and seemed confused, as if searching for an answer.

Then she looked out the window again and said "She used to love this little diary-room. She used to look out at that beautiful garden, feel the sun on her, and dream of what it would be like to be single again…"

"Did she write that in her diary?" asked Jenny, still totally enthralled, and ignoring her husband's remark.

The guide looked confused again, as if she didn't understand the point of the question, and said after frowning for a few moments "No".

"Then how can you know what she was daydreaming about?".

Once again there was a look of confusion on the guide's face.

"Because I know her so well…..everything about her……" she said eventually.

The she leaned over and read more,

"The beauty of having my husband and the children away is I don't have to wear gloves. When they are here I wear them because I can't abide touching anything they might have touched. When they are gone I scrub thoroughly all the bannisters, all the door handles, all the chairs, and anything else their filthy little hands might have touched, then I throw away the cloths I used, and I can take off my gloves and walk around bare-handed…"

Jenny then pointed to a pair of delicate white ladies' gloves in a flat glass case beside the diary.

"Are those her gloves?" she enquired of the guide.

The guide surveyed them thoughtfully, then said "Evelyn couldn't bear to touch anything her children might have touched, so she wore these white gloves constantly, except when her husband had taken the children away from home……."

"I think that's called Obsessive Compulsive Disorder" remarked Chris in a matter-of-fact tone, interrupting her.

"Oh, you're into your big words again, are you?" protested Jenny. "She put her hand on the guide's arm. "Don't worry about him, dear, He never wanted to come in here in the first place."

But the guide stopped reading to stare out the window again as if Chris's words had set her thinking.

'She must have had very small hands" Jenny then remarked, looking at the gloves.

The guide looked back from the window, and down at the pair of gloves, and then placed her hand over the glass above one of the gloves. It matched the size of the glove exactly.

"Yes" she said softly. "She did have very small hands…very small, delicate hands….how could those little hands have harmed anyone?"

Then she snapped out of her reverie and a playful glint came into her eye. "Step back into the hallway and then keep on walking" she said to them. They did so and walked on a few paces, and the guide said "I'm going to play a trick on you. Keep looking forward, don't look back at me."

They did as she told them, and suddenly they heard a scamper of feet, turned round, and she was gone. But then they heard footsteps behind the wall to the left of them, and then below them, and then above them and then to the other side of them, and then from where, well, they just couldn't tell, and then suddenly a door burst open at the other end of the hall, and the guide burst out throwing her hands wide and beaming.

"Di-da!!" She bowed as if she was taking an encore on a stage. Then she resumed her old stance with her hands clasped in front of her and her feet pointing outwards.

"I warned you this was a real rabbit warren of a house! I just wanted to prove it!"

"A secret passage?" exclaimed Jenny. "I love secret passages. I wish we had one in our house!"

"No!. But there ways and means of getting around here that only I know! But come and let me show you the childrens' room"

She led them further on down the hall, then up some stairs, and into a large room that had a cot, one simple single bed, a larger canopied bed and a low table with small, childrens' chairs around it, a small blackboard, a small school desk, a bookcase, and all sorts of childrens' toys of the period, including a magnificent carved rocking horse.

The guide started picking up toys and talking about them. "These were the building blocks. The boys loved these! They would build castles, and forts, and grand houses, and barns and mountains, and bridges and all sorts of things…they were very clever…"

Then the guide looked sideways slyly at Chris and Jenny. "And then Evelyn liked to come in and knock them all down! So they'd have to start all over again!"

She opened her mouth and laughed, and for the first time Chris and Jenny saw she had a mouthful of rotting and broken teeth.

Chris nodded and looked round the rest of the room. "Fruit loop!" he said again, but somehow Jenny was only more fascinated and remarked. "She sounds like a real character!"

Then the guide looked down at Bobby, still clinging to Jenny's dress and looking at the guide with the same horror. "So it wasn't any point building them in the first place, was it?".

Then she walked over to the magnificent rocking horse, obviously hand-carved. It was so big the top of its head was just about at the same level as hers.

"The children loved this as well" she said. Then a cloud seemed to come over her face. "Their father, George Hardy, made it himself. He was a master with his hands". She said it with a kind of resentment, as if it was hurtful to her to admit the possession by him of any sort of talent. She ran her hands over the horse, and indeed it was carved as nearly as possible to resemble hair and the bone structure of a real horse.

Then she brightened up and looked at Bobby.

"Would you like this horse, Bobby?" she said.

As if he was afraid not to answer her, Bobby said plaintively "Yes"

She bent slightly and leaned down towards him. Her voice suddenly took on a tone of vicious spite. "Well, you can't have it! And Evelyn didn't want her children to use it! Because it was made by her husband. And whenever she found them riding on it…!"

For a second a storm cloud of anger passed over her face, then she was back to her engaging smile.

She continued to walk around the room, picking up and talking about various weird and wonderful toys and games that the children had, and in every case there was some complicated story why if their mother happened to be around they never really got the proper use out of them due to a whim of Evelyn's.

Then she led them out and back into the corridor and into the next room. "This is the master bedroom" she announced.

It was a large room, with a magnificent four-poster double bed with sumptuous curtains that could be drawn all around it. The extravagant nature of the furnishings indicated that it was intended there should be no other bedroom in the house that could equal it. But for some reason the guide, as she walked up to the bed and stood by it, wore a rather a dubious expression. The bed was so high it was above her waist.

"That wouldn't be any good for someone your size" commented Jenny. You'd be hard put to climb into it!"

In answer, the guide raised her finger as if to make a point, and pulled over a small chest that was next to the bed. She pulled out what looked like a drawer, but was revealed to be a small set of steps that folded down. She pulled it up to the bed, and promptly walked up it and jumped onto the bed, where she lay flat on her back with her arms outstretched and her feet apart.

"This was where Evelyn and George slept. Though Evelyn used to prefer to go up and lie on the roof in the summer under the stars, or even go out and lie in the garden and talk to the trees. ...When he was away she would le for hours like this, glorying in the feeling of being alone...."

She seemed to go into a reverie, then she suddenly sat up, with a sly grin on her face, and pulled all the curtains round her. They waited, and there was just silence.

"What's she doing?" Jenny whispered to Chris.

"Perhaps she's undressing" suggested Chris facetiously, curling his lip as if that wasn't something he relished the idea of seeing.

Then suddenly the French windows that led to a balcony opened and the guide stepped from there into the room. Jenny's jaw dropped. "How on earth did you get out there?"

But the guide simply said as if there nothing untoward "And sometimes instead of going down into the garden Evelyn would go out and lie on the balcony on hot nights under the stars, especially if George had been in the liquors.

"But come with me so I can show you the grand ballroom."

They followed her out, Jenny gaping, Chris frowning, and went down another flight of stairs into another hallway and came into a room that was larger than any of the ones they had been in and even more ornate. There were magnificent chandeliers hanging from the ceiling A heavy, gilt picture rail ran all the way around. The ceiling was domed with skylights round the edge of the dome. The wallpaper was sumptuous. There were heavily carved and ornate chairs around the perimeter of the room. There was a magnificent mirror about ten feet long and six feet high hanging from one wall in a massive gilt frame. Opposite was a peculiar kind of small stage projecting from the wall about halfway up.

"This was the grand ballroom, where dances and entertainment were staged" explained the guide, standing right in the middle of the floor for effect. "Take a look at this wonderful mirror"

She indicated an enormous mirror with a heavy, gilt frame hanging off the wall.

"It took four men to lift into place. Imagine how wonderfully the images of the dancers as they came and went in all their finery reflected in the mirror. And look at the figures carved all way round the frame. They tell a story". Chris and Jenny stood in front of it following the carving round with their eyes, trying to decipher what the story was.. Suddenly the guide's voice seemed to come from somewhere behind but above them.

They turned and she was standing in the peculiar "stage" that jutted out from the wall opposite the mirror, like the box at a theatre. They hadn't heard her move, and she seemed to have got up there in a remarkably short space of time.

"And this is where the orchestra played. They would have a trio of two stringed instruments, usually a cello and a violin, and a flute, and the music would waft over the heads of the dancers, and reverberate round the dome of this magnificent room."

"How on earth did you get up there so quickly?" asked Jenny.

The guide pointed to the doorway, then moved her arm in a circle to indicate there was a way up into the "stage" if you went out that door and turned left.

"The musicians didn't drag their instruments through the ballroom" she explained. "They had their own entrance".

"But how did you get up there in such a short apace of time?" insisted Jenny. "And we didn't even hear you."

The guide only beamed at her with a look that seemed to challenge her to find her own explanation.

"I am quick! And I can be very silent!"

"You weren't silent when you were showing off that secret passage."

The guide raised her eyebrows and gave Jenny another peculiar smile as if to say again "I challenge you then to work out why that is!"

"Evelyn had a favourite song she liked the orchestra to play, Greensleeves" she went on. "But her husband, George Hardy, insisted they couldn't play that all evening just to please her, so when her husband and children were away, she used to pay the orchestra to come back, sit up here, and play Greensleeves over and over for hours on end, while she just sat in the middle of the room on one of those chairs listening to it!

"Unfortunately she was rather overweight and short and quite clumsy, so she wasn't built for dancing, but she loved to listen to that song. Sometimes she would just sing along with it while they played, and sometimes she would just listen, moving her foot up and down in time to the music."

"For hours on end…the same tune…?" repeated Chris, as if he wanted to confirm he had heard right.

"Yes. She loved that tune!" explained the guide.

Chris turned away to look at the rest of the room again and remarked again, with an air of great finality "A total fruit loop!".

"How do you know that about Greensleeves?" asked Jenny. "Did she put in her diary?"

The guide looked into the distance with the same wistful look she exhibited when she seemed to be debating how to answer a question.

"No, she never wrote that in her diary" she murmured dreamily.

"Did someone write her biography?"

This made the guide give a little laugh.

"No".

"Well how do you know it?"

The guide suddenly looked confused again, and seemed to be debating within herself how to answer, until she said

"I know it, because … I know it…That's all"

She ran her hand round the inside of her collar again, then rubbed her left wrist with her right hand,

and her right wrist with her left hand, then suddenly snapped back out of it, and exclaimed

"I must show you the cellar! Go out through that door" she pointed to the end of the ballroom "opposite to where you came in!".

They walked out, and into another hallway, then the guide appeared from a doorway on the right. By now they were so used to her disappearing and then reappearing from nowhere they didn't remark on it. She led them down some wooden stairs that had two flights, opened a door, and they were in the cellars.

"This was George Hardy's favourite part of the house' she said, when they were all down, and her voice echoed back off the cold stone walls that surrounded them. "Because this was where he kept his wine, and his spirits, and his beer. Sometimes he would come down here to drink, and get so drunk he couldn't walk back upstairs. That suited Evelyn, of course, because....." the guide suddenly lowered her eyes, and looked very introspective, and took her typical pose with her hands clasped in front of her "......because if he came upstairs in that state, there was no knowing what evil he might perpetrate on her and his children."

Chris and Jenny looked round, The cellars were extensive and divided into several alcoves, with curved archways. There were racks of empty wine bottles, and large empty barrels on their sides to simulate what they would have looked like 150 years ago. There was a sensation of coldness, and dampness, and mustiness.

"So he had what we call these days 'a drinking problem', then" opined Chris.

The guide looked at him as if she thought he was being flippant. "He was a bad man at the best of times, and the liquors only made him worse".

She then turned, lifted her skirt so she wouldn't catch it, and started back up the steps.

While Chris and Jenny went to follow her, Chris made a motion of holding his nose and pointing at her back, and Jenny shrugged and nodded in answer. "Have you noticed how she stinks" Chris hissed to her. "I think she never changes out of that dress!"

When they got back to the hallway the guide said "I want to show you the day room. This was Evelyn spent a lot of her time, when she wasn't writing her diary."

"Or wrecking the kids' toys" chipped in Chris.

They walked in to the dayroom. It was a sumptuously furnished, large rectangular room, lit by an enormous bay window that wend right down to the floor at one end. It had more natural light than any other room they had been in. There were folding tables where cards could be played, a spinning wheel, a tapestry frame, a sewing table, and a very antique square-shaped piano.

"This is where Evelyn used to spend her afternoons" the guide explained. "The children were banned from this room. It was her room. Only the servants were allowed to come in to dust it, or bring anything she required. She loved to spin on the wheel, and do tapestry, or knit, or sometimes just read, and sometimes play solitaire with herself, and sometimes" she looked doubtfully at the piano "play music"

She surveyed the piano for a few more moments and then said. "This is very different from a modern piano. It can't be properly tuned, because the frame is wooden, and if the strings were stretched to concert pitch the frame would break, and it wouldn't stay tuned anyway."

"Do you play?" asked Jenny.

The guide seemed to debate the point within herself, then in answer to Jenny's question she sat down on the stool, and gingerly put her fingers on the keys, and played, in a sort of hesitating, fumbling way, like a child who has just succeeded in learning one tune "Greensleeves" Then she played it again. Then she played it again. Then she sunk back and stared at the instrument sullenly.

"As you can hear, it doesn't sound anything like a modern piano, or even sound as it would have one hundred and fifty years ago, due to being so worn and out of tune" she bemoaned.

"Play something else" urged Jenny cheerily.

But the guide just sat looking mournfully at the instrument.

"That's all I can play" she said finally. "But I like that song so much …It's the only song I want to play. Why should I play other tunes if I like only that one? I just wish the piano sounded as sweet and melodious as it did 150 years ago…."

Something just occurred to Jenny. "Evelyn seems to have been a rather solitary person. Didn't she have friends that came and visited her?" she inquired.

The guide looked into the distance with the dreamy, ambiguous look again, ran her fingers round inside her collar, rubbed her wrists, and said "The people in the village were very strange, the ladies, and the men, all were very strange. Every one of them. Evelyn tried, but she couldn't befriend them. They were ……….just very strange…… not like her… not like her at all…very strange….."

"Well, not everyone's as normal as Evelyn was" said Chris sarcastically.

But in answer, Evelyn only looked into the distance through the French windows and nodded, and said, as if the sarcasm was lost on her, "Quite…quite….".

"I don't know how you remember all this you've told us" said Jenny. "You must have spent hours being taught this history"

The guide looked back and said carelessly "Nobody taught me".

"Then how do you know it?"

Once again they saw that dreamy look in her eyes as she looked away as if debating how she should answer the question.

"I...I know it because....this house...is in my bones!"

She turned and looked at them slyly.

"You're really enjoying this tour, aren't you?" she asked them.

"Loving it!" said Jenny enthusiastically, beaming at her and putting her hand on the guide's arm. Chris just looked at her blankly, trying to indicate to her without saying that he thought she was quite mad.

The guide reached into a pocket in her dress and took out an enormous old-fashioned key.

"There's something that's not really open for public viewing that I'd still love you to see. Follow me"

She led them out, and a little way further down the hall, put the key in the lock of a door, and turned it. The door opened and she pushed it inwards.

"Follow me up these stairs, but be very careful!"

She lifted her skirts so she wouldn't trip, and proceeded up a very rickety spiral staircase that was in a stairwell so dark they could hardly see. Chris had to bend his head the clearance was so low. They went up one storey, and turned 360 degrees around at the same time, then the guide opened a door at the top, and a patch more light filtered in.

They were in an attic, where Chris could only stand up in the centre, as the roof sloped away to the floor at all sides.

"Don't step anywhere I don't, because it's not safe" the guide warned. "This was used as servants' quarters. The poor servants. You can imagine how hot it was in here in the middle of summer, and how cold in the winter with the chilly wind blowing through the cracks between the shingles in the roof. Can't you imagine a pair of young servant girls swapping secrets about their lives and loves, or crying themselves to sleep with dejection at their lowly lot in life, or hugging each other to keep warm in the depths of winter?"

Jenny looked round, as if she could well imagine how it must have been.

Then the guide looked at Bobby, clinging to his mother's skirt and staring at the guide with a fearful look "And of course, sometimes it was used as place to lock up bad children if they had been very naughty and needed to be taught a lesson!".

At this Bobby burst into tears.

Jenny hugged him to her legs to comfort him. "Don't worry, dear, the lady's only joking. There, there. there, there, she's only having a little joke. No one's going to lock you up here. We'll be out soon".

The guide only surveyed Bobby as if she found his histrionics amusing. For the first time Jenny looked at her with some annoyance.

Then the guide turned and opened another door that was cut into the roof. "Follow me out here" she said.

They bent their heads, and went through the low doorway and found themselves in bright sunlight on the roof of the house, on a small flat space like a balcony with battlements all along the edge. It was quite breezy, but they had a magnificent view. But they were shocked when the guide stepped backwards without even looking where she was placing her feet, onto the top of one of the battlements, with the agility of a gymnast, and stood with her back to the sheer drop behind her, and clasped her hands in front of her as if she was going to make a speech. The back of her heels were right at the edge of the battlement.

"Oh my gosh" exclaimed Jenny putting her hands to each side of her face. "Be careful dear! That's a three storey drop behind you!"

She clasped Bobby too her. "Stay with me Bobby, don't you dare go near the edge".

The guide just smiled and looked as if it was not a worry to her. "I can't fall. And what's that they say? 'You can only die once!'"

She turned half round and waved her hand at the view.

"Isn't it magnificent? From here on a clear day they could see ships at sea, and they used to signal to them with a system of flags to tell them if they needed supplies, or if they had to come into the wharf to be picked up. And they could spot bushfires miles and miles away."

The skirt of her dark blue dress blew around her in the wind and she held her hair back as the wind blew it across her face, as she contemplated the distance wistfully.

"Can you see the sea out there through the trees?" she asked, pointing over their heads.

Chris and Jenny turned round looked where she was pointing and could just make out the sea. They had their back to her. Then suddenly her voice seemed to come from down low. They turned and the guide was lying flat on her back with her hands behind her head. They hadn't heard her step down off the battlements.

"Lady of the house Evelyn, used to come up here sometimes on the hot nights, or when she had had a fight with her husband George, for relief and just lie under the stars and sing herself to sleep" said the guide, dreamily.

"Did she sing Greensleeves?" suggested Chris, sarcastically. But the guide ignored him.

"Was that in the diary, about singing herself to sleep?" asked Jenny.

The guide looked up at her confused.

"No"

"Then how do you know she did it?" pursued Jenny.

Once again they that troubled look on her face, as if she was debating something within herself. Then she ran her hand round inside her collar again, and stroked each wrist with the other hand in turn again as if they were sore.

"I just …know..".she muttered finally.

Chris and Jenny turned to look at the distant sea again. Then they heard the guide's voice right behind them. They turned and she was standing up again. They hadn't heard her rise.

"Is this from where the awful Evelyn threw her children?" asked Jenny.

A look of shock came over the guide's face, and she looked Jenny up and down. "Who told you that she did?" she asked.

"Why, Carol. She said Evelyn took her children up on the roof and threw them off, and then ran down-stairs drowned them in a pond when she saw they weren't quite dead"

"It's a lie!" the guide said in a strident tone with a look of extreme displeasure on her face, and an air of authority. She looked into the distance. "She was wrongly accused, and hanged for crimes she didn't commit. Her husband, George Hardy, was a bad, bad man. He came in a fit of rage once …intoxicated out of his mind ….and.." she put her hands to her face, as if in horror "....he took the three beautiful little children... and he dragged them up to the attic. here ....and he took them out on these battlements ...and he...... threw them off! But when he ran down the stairs to see if they were dead, they weren't dead! They were just rolling on the ground screaming with all their bones broken screaming, so he dragged them to the creek, and he held both their heads under the water, until they were dead!...... And then his wife, the adoring, faithful, pious, devoted, gentle Evelyn, who heard the screams.. came running out...and saw what he had done...she went to attack him..tried to beat him with her tiny fists .. but he threw her on the ground...then he tried to choke her..but she fought herself free...because he was so drunk, even though he was so strong .... he was not able to hold her..and she picked up an axe to defend herself" suddenly the guide made motions as if she herself had an axe in her hand and was swinging it "...and she struck him..and she struck him..and struck him.....until he was dead. ...But they wouldn't believe her...the servants lied and said they had seen it all and she had killed the children, and then killed her husband.. because he had tried to stop her....! So she was tried..and convicted.. of killing her own children..and her husband ..and she was taken..."

here she suddenly made the motion again of running her hand round inside her collar as if it was choking her."..to a place not far from here....and hanged!...And the rope was too short and she took many, many minutes to die... hanging there choking and struggling..and twisting and turning..with her hands tied behind her.." She suddenly started the other motion of stroking each of her wrists with the opposite hand in turn, as if they were hurting."…..until finally she expired..Oh what a miscarriage of justice! She loved her three little children…like no mother had even loved her children ….and she was killed for their killing…but she was not guilty! Oh what a miscarriage of justice…!"

All the time she alternately made the motion of running her hand around inside her collar, pulling it away from her neck, and stroking her wrists.

When she had finished her diatribe, she stared at the stone floor of the balcony for many seconds with a look of terror on her face, while Chris and Jenny stood stock still in horror. Then, as suddenly, the guide's demeanour changed, and she smiled.

"We'll go back downstairs now" she said.

As she led then back into the attic and down the rickety stairs she called back "Be careful again, these stairs are very dangerous, I can tell you." Then as if on an afterthought, she added, looking down at

Bobby, who was coming down the stairs behind her holding his mother's hand "That's another way we used to punish naughty children, we used to throw them down the attic stairs and break all their bones!"

Bobby looked up at her in fear, and as she went to tousle his hair he pulled away

When they were back down the stairs, and she had locked the door that led to the attic, Jenny said "You seem to know this place like the back of your hand!"

The guide stood still and stared dreamily past the Jenny's face. "Every inch of it. Every corner, Every stair of every staircase. Every door. Every nook and cranny. Every creaking floorboard. Every window-shutter that rattles in the wind. Every cobweb. Every knot in the planks of wood. I can find my way even in the dark, when the candle blows out, and I haven't a match to re-light it.."

"Why on earth would you be using a candle when there are lights?"

Once again they saw the peculiar ambiguous look on her face. She frowned, looked down, then left and right, then looked half up, and past them, as if debating something within herself.

"Oh yes….. there are lights now, aren't there….."

Then she came out of her reverie and said "I ought to know it well, as I live here"

Jenny looked confused. "Wait a minute, what do you mean you 'live here?' You told us you come and go through your private entrance. Surely you don't actually live here"

The guide narrowed her eyes slightly, and looked suddenly very evasive, as if she was debating within herself what to say by way of explanation.

"I live here…..sometimes…" she explained. "So I can get…the feel of the place….and be a better guide……But I can also come and go as I please, as I said".

Jenny studied the guide's face closely as if trying to fathom this strange creature.

"Well, I guess you would never have any trouble being late for work if you slept here overnight!" she finally opined. "Where do you sleep? In the grand bedroom?"

The guide just looked at her with the same inscrutable expression, then looked past her into the distance. "I can sleep anywhere I like…sometimes I don't sleep…I just walk all through the house… making sure everything is safe….." She ran her fingers round inside her collar again, and winced slightly, "talking to the house…."

Then she snapped out of it, and said "Now we'll go to the East Wing. To get there we have to go through the entrance hall where we started from."

She opened a door, and they found themselves back in the hallway where they had come in.

"And here we are back in the grand entrance hall" said the guide.

Chris took his cue.

"Good, That means we're finished and we can go!"

At this a look of horror came over the guide's face. "Oh, please don't go, I haven't shown you one tenth of the house! That door there goes to the East Wing, where George Hardy's study is, and the servants quarters, and I want to take you out and show you the barns, and the quarters above them where the stable hands lived, and the garden, and the pond, and the kitchen.....the kitchen is separate from the house, across the courtyard, to protect the rest of the house from fire......... You haven't seen one half of this place. You haven't heard a fraction of the tales. There's so many stories, so any treasures, so many memories, so many secrets, so many characters,,,," Her voice became more and more strident and pleading with each word.

Jenny put her hand lightly on the guide's arm as if to calm her. "We know, love, but we have to go. I could stay here all day listening to you, but we have to be somewhere" she explained. "We'll be back...."

"But I only live....I feel like I only live .... while there are people I can show the house to, and want to see it, and trust me..." the guide appealed to them plaintively. "This is my life. I feel like I only come alive while people are wandering through the house, and thinking about the house, and listening to me.....I only live while the past is in peoples' minds....I only live while I am telling people my stories......Can't you stay even a short while longer....?"

Chris said with a surly tone "No, we have to go"

"You must come back at night, sometime, and I can show you through by candlelight! The flickering light of the candle shows up nooks and crannies you never knew were existed, and casts shadows in the most amazing shapes. By candlelight is the only real way to know the house. Everything else is false. In candlelight the house actually comes alive..it talks to you.. it creaks and moans and groans as you walk through it..it talks to you in its own language.....and I know exactly what it's saying. I speak the house-language. I talk back to it, and then it talks back to me. ..It's a friendly house, it wouldn't harm you, unless you try to harm it Then woe-betide you....Oh, do come back one day ...The house likes you...I can tell it likes you....It wants you to come back...I can feel the house whispering to me it wants you back ....."

"Thank you, we've seen everything" said Chris, in a tone that really meant "The place gives me the creeps by daylight, do you think I want to see it by candlelight?"

"I'll twist his arm" said Jenny, lightly touching the guide again on her forearm, Then as she did so, she took her hand away, and frowned for a second. But then she said "I promise you. I'll talk him round."

They walked out and round the corner into the front office. They had to blink to get accustomed to the light. Then, just as they came out, Jenny turned and said, looking at Chris in earnest

"We should thank her, you know. We never even thanked her". She turned and went back in, but though she looked left and right, the guide was gone. She had disappeared as quickly as she had made her entrance.

Then Jenny suddenly realised thy hadn't even asked the guide's name. "Hallo! Hallo!" she called, but there was no answer. "Thank you for a lovely tour, wherever you are!" she added, but there was no answer.

She came back out to Chris.

"She's gone!"

Jenny went straight up to Carol at the desk "Well, your guide was there after all. And we had a most interesting tour. But she is a bit of a strange one. I don't know which was most interesting, the tour or the guide!"

Carol looked up and frowned.

"What are you talking about? I told you she's not in today. In fact, I've just been on the phone to her. She lying in bed totally zonked out with the 'flu!"

"But there was a guide there" insisted Jenny. "She gave us a tour all round the house. And a fascinating tour it was! Mind you, not as fascinating as she was! She is quite a character!"

"What did this….. 'person'…… look like?"

"She was short, and dumpy, very pale skin, and dark hair tied behind….."

"And broken teeth, fleas and terrible body odour" added Chris as if he was anxious the full facts of the case should be filled in.

"Well our guide is a big woman" said Carol. She put her hands out to indicate her girth. "And tall, nearly six feet! She wears caftans to hide her size." She shrugged, and looked back down at her work. "Maybe someone walked in off the street and decided to impersonate a guide. But I've been here all the time, no-one came past"

"She said she had a secret entrance" pursued Jenny.

Carol looked up starting to get a little impatient. "There's no 'secret entrance'".

"Perhaps she climbed in through a window!" suggested Chris, thinking the whole thing was a farcical joke anyway, and with an air that he didn't care one way or another.

"The windows are all locked, for security reasons".

"Perhaps she came down the chimney" suggested Chris further, grinning.

Jenny looked at him with a sarcastic expression. "Yes, she looked like she was all covered in soot and coal dust, didn't you notice?"

She turned to Carol. "Actually, she said sometimes, she lives here".

Carol looked as if she was becoming even more impatient. "Lives here? No-one lives here"

"She even took us up into the attic!" Jenny said to Carol.

Now Carol shook her head most peremptorily.

"She couldn't have. It's locked. It's only under special circumstances is anyone is allowed up there, because for one thing the floor is not safe, and the stairs are quite dangerous. It's not open to the general public. We're having work done on it. It won't be open to the public again for months"

"But she had a key to the stairwell that leads up there!"

Carol shook her head again, and opened a draw to her right and took out an old key just like the guide had used.

"This is the only key here to the attic. The only copy is kept in a safe at another location, for security! Whoever was showing you round couldn't have had a key to the attic!"

Jenny persisted. "And she knew a secret passage that let her disappear at one end of the hallway that goes past the bedrooms and reappear the other end".

Carol looked like she was getting annoyed.

"There's no secret passage" she said bluntly, as if her word was final.

"But there is, we heard her footsteps behind the wall, and then above us and below us, and then she reappeared"

"The house has been gone over with a fine-toothed comb during restoration so everything that needed replacing could be replaced, and every piece of the structure has been catalogued and photographed and documented. There's no secret passages!"

But Jenny was defiant.

"If there was a secret passage, you wouldn't know about it anyway, because it was secret!" she proudly proclaimed as if that was final. Then she turned away to look at the photographs on the wall.

She was looking at the framed pictures of the family. Suddenly she stopped in front of one and, pointing at it, exclaimed "That's her! That's her! That's the lady who was showing us round!" She looked round at Carol, then back at the photograph to study it even closer. "It's even the very same dress"

"Well, now you're really in another timezone" said Carol. "That's the infamous Evelyn, the mistress of the house. Evelyn Hardy. The one who was hanged for murdering her own three little children and her husband!"

"But the guide told us George Hardy was a terrible man and a drunk. She said he'd go down to the cellars and drink so much he couldn't get back up the stairs."

"If he drank, it would be to forget what he was married to" said Carol." Actually there's no record he was a heavy drinker.

"He might have shut himself down there with the children a few times to protect himself from his wife when she was in one of her tantrums!"

But even though the photo was old and fuzzy, there was no mistaking the face, and the pose, and the dress. Jenny looked at Carol insistently.

"But that's the woman who was showing us around! That's even the very same dress she wore!"

Carol got up and took a key from the drawer at the side. She walked over to a door that was the other side of her desk to the entrance to the house. The door had frosted glass on its top half that said MUSEUM. As she unlocked the door and opened it and turned on a the light inside she said "You mean this one?"

The light was dim, but as they walked in after her they saw a wire dummy in a glass case clad in the very same dress their guide had been wearing. Jenny let out a little scream and cupped her hand to her mouth.

"This is the museum room, we're renovating it, so it's generally locked at the present time and not for public view. This was Evelyn's dress" said Carol "They say she was actually hanged in it, which seems a bit weird, but that's the legend".

Jenny walked round the case gaping at the dress, examining it closely.

"It's kept in this constant climactic conditions and dim light to stop it deteriorating because it's so fragile due to its great age"

"That's the dress she was wearing" said Jenny. "It the very same dress!. Look, you see how her lace cuff on the left hand slide is slightly torn – that's just how hers was!"

She looked at Carol.

"She must have come in here and taken it out!" pursued Jenny.

Carol shook her head. "She couldn't have. The cabinet is locked, and as you can see the room is locked, and if you were even to handle that dress, parts of it would just disintegrate. It's in a very delicate condition now. When fabric is 100 years old, and it has been well worn before that…it will just fall to pieces if not handled with the utmost care. Even excessive sunlight will destroy it"

Jenny couldn't take her eyes of the dress, until the girl from the desk led them out and turned off the light

As she sat down at her desk again she said "You know there is a woman in the town who dresses like that. She's a descendent of the family, but only by marriage, she's not a blood relation at all, but she calls herself Evelyn. She's mentally retarded and does nothing but walk around town all day in an old dress just like that one, grunting and making faces at people, and abusing them, and sometimes even throwing things at them, and shoplifting".

"Then that's her!" said Chris. "She must have sneaked in here somehow and given us the tour!"

Carol shook her head. "It couldn't be her. Number one, no-one can 'sneak in' and number two she can't put two words together to make a sentence. She's banned from here anyway. She's literally an imbecile. When she does appear on the streets she just runs round all day in that old dress muttering gibberish and abusing people.

"Actually, I say mutter, but she doesn't as much mutter as grunt. Thankfully we don't often see her….

"Actually you often smell her before you see her. I don't think she ever changes her clothes or washes, and pongs like anything."

Chris looked at Jenny meaningfully. Then Chris started walking out the door.

"We've got to go now, anyway. We're late already".

"Thank you for your help, anyway" said Jenny, taking Bobby's hand as they went out of the front doorway and back down the drive to the carpark.

"I don't like that lady" squealed Bobby when they were a fair way from the house.

"That's all right" his father said, consoling him. "We won't be coming back here"

Jenny was frowning and deep in thought. Suddenly she stopped, which made Chris stop as well. She stood in front of him and looked up at her husband.

"You know what we've seen?"

"Yeah, a raving nut-case!"

"No!. We've seen a ghost! We've been given a tour of the house by a ghost! That guide was Evelyn! Didn't you notice she appeared straight after I called out the spirits of the house? She heard me, and she came!

"That dress fitted her exactly, exactly! It couldn't have been made for someone else 100 years ago, unless she was that someone else! The length was exactly right! The length of the sleeves was exactly right! The shoulders were exactly right! The waist was exactly right! The neck was exactly right – even though she kept trying to loosen it – it wasn't tight, and it wasn't too loose. And as she said, she went in and out at all the wrong places, and so did the dress, the dress went in and out all the places she did! Do you know the chance a dress like that would fit exactly just someone who happened to walk in off the street to work as a guide 100 years later? It's one chance in a million. That dress was made to fit"

"So? They had it made just to fit her!"

"Had it made? Did you see it? It was old as the hills, it was well preserved, but it was rubbed and stretched and worn with use. It couldn't get so rubbed and worn just walking round in it a few hours for a few days a week. The lace was yellowed with age. And the whole dress was hand stitched! I know stitching, and I know dress making - you couldn't even get a materials like that now – you wouldn't even get anyone who could do the stitching! And why would you hand stitch a dress when we have machines?

"And her hands were exactly the same size as Evelyn's gloves. That's because she was Evelyn!"

"So? She had small hands" disagreed Chris. "Lots of women have small hands".

But Jenny persisted. "And did you notice how she knew the entire contents of the diary, without reading it? It could only mean one thing - she wrote it herself It was her diary!"

"Perhaps she memorised it"

"And all the anecdotes and history of the family and the house. She said no-one taught her. That's because she knew it already."

"Perhaps she was lying. I think she's a total fruit loop anyway. This Evelyn was a fruit loop, and so is she. By the time it was over she was giving me the creeps. And I'll tell you another thing - ghosts don't have substance. You can't touch them and feel them!. If you reach out your hand to feel them, your hand just goes right through them."

"Oh, you're an expert on ghosts now?"

"I'm telling you, they don't have substance. They're ethereal!"

"That's a big word for someone like you".

He just scowled in impatient annoyance and went on. "She picked up Bobby. I felt her when she put her hand on my arm Her hand was warm. She was flesh and blood!"

Jenny countered "Well, when I touched her she was cold. And why was Bobby so scared of her?"

"Because she kept talking about locking children in the cellar and throwing them down the stairs! Can you blame him? Anyway, there's no accounting for why kids like or don't like someone."

"But he's never reacted to anyone like that! You know..they say children know…they have instinct….. intuition…that adults don't have …they can tell the people that want to harm them…And if she murdered her own children….."

She shuddered suddenly at the thought a murderer had picked up Bobby.

"Perhaps he didn't like her teeth!" said Chris, dismissively. "Did you see them?"

"Yes. Half of them were missing. And the one that were left were all broken and rotten!" She poked Chris in the ribs by way of emphasis. "In the old days people had bad teeth – that's why you never see people smiling in an old photograph - the people never have their mouths open, because they had to hide their rotten teeth!"

"So she had bad teeth. There's plenty of people walking round with bad teeth!"

"In this day and age? Like that? If people have bad teeth these days, they get them fixed! And what about the fleas! That's what people had in the old days!

"And do you remember she said, while she was standing on the battlements 'You only die once'? She said that - because she had already died. And the way she stood there, right on the edge. No normal person could do that without flinching!"

"Well, she wasn't a normal person. She was nuts, I keep telling you, that's all"

"No! She was a ghost! That's why she wasn't afraid of falling!"

"She was nuts! What about when she was talking about locking bad children in the attic and pushing them down the stairs, and locking them in the cellar and breaking their toys. Bobby was scared stiff. Normal people don't talk like that. I don't know why they'd let someone like that loose on the public. They must be desperate for staff"

"But she wasn't staff! Carol said the guide was away. She didn't know anything about her.

"And how was she able to disappear and re-appear if she wasn't a ghost? How did she slip out from the curtains of that four poster bed and get onto the balcony without us seeing?"

"She slipped out the other side of the bed that we couldn't see because of the curtains, there was another door behind, and that door led to the balcony...somehow" said Chris, but not very convincingly. "How do you think magicians make cards appear out of their sleeves? They just have a way of doing it, that's all".

Jenny then looked into the distance and smiled thoughtfully, as if she didn't have any more answers for him, but was still convinced, until she said "Well, she was a harmless ghost. It didn' t matter what she said. She couldn't hurt anyone.

"But I tell you something, when I put my hand on her arm, just as we were leaving, did you notice me pull away? I pulled away because her arm was cold as ice. She might have felt warm when you touched her, but there was no warmth at all coming through the sleeve of her dress when I touched her that last time. It was like the sleeve of the dress had been pulled over a sculptured block of ice."

"Poor circulation!" suggested Chris.

"No" insisted Jenny. "That's just another thing proves we've been taken round that house by a ghost.

"And I tell you something else, did you notice she ponged something awful. Like she hadn't washed in weeks?"

"So? She had what they call "poor personal hygiene"".

"Do you think a person like that would be allowed to come into work? She'd be told to go home and clean herself up. Someone would have complained. You see, that's another thing they did in those days, They never washed. And the fleas – in those days people did have fleas

"And did you notice she acted like she'd never seen a modern camera before? And she didn't know what 'take pictures' meant? And she asked us 'Weren't the horses tired?' And she talked about using candles....."

"Okay, but the whole house was lit with electric light, she didn't question that, and our clothes are modern clothes, they weren't like the clothes they wore in those days, she didn't say 'Why are you dressed like that?' If she'd never seen a modern camera, why wasn't she surprised by modern clothes and electric light? It doesn't make sense. She was play-acting, 'The horses must be tired'" He imitated her tone scornfully. "But her act wasn't complete – there were holes in it you could walk through. She stuffed up!"

Jenny heard him out with a thoughtful but piqued look. Then she suggested in a tone like she was clutching at straws "Maybe she was a ghost with a sense of humour."

Then her voice changed back to one of confidence, her mind was made up. "No, I don't believe she did kill her children. I believe it was her husband. And she was taken before her time, and that's why her spirit lingers on to tell the world at any chance she can how she was wronged It's like I said before we went in, when people are taken before their time, they refuse to leave the earth completely, they linger on, in the places they inhabited, to seek justice, and I'm a very spiritual person, by going into her house, I conjured her back from the dead....I had a feeling about that place, when I saw it from the road...we were meant to go in, and we were meant to meet Evelyn, so we can tell the world, about how she was wronged, and her spirit can finally rest in peace....."

Chris only made a dismissive noise of contempt.

They started walking towards the car again. They got in and drove back to the town. But when they got to the village Jenny insisted "Stop somewhere. I just feel like I'd like to buy some sort of souvenir of this place, something to remember our visit by. I didn't see anything I wanted at the house. There must be a souvenir shop somewhere".

They got out and wandered along the shops. It seemed strange to be back in the sunlight and the 21st century after the dimness and shadows of The Old House. They stopped at the window of a gift and souvenir shop, where all sorts of gaudy trinkets relating to the town were being sold.

Suddenly Jenny screamed and pointed into the window. "Look!".

There was a little doll about six inches high, dressed in a dark blue long dress, laced cuffs and laced collar, with her hands tied behind her actually swinging from a gallows.

Jenny pushed open the door and rushed in.

There was a very well groomed lady behind the counter with an unmistakable air about her of being the shop owner "Can we see that gruesome little doll you have in the window, the one swinging from a gallows?" Jenny said to her.

The shop owner made a peculiar face as if to say "That dreadful thing - If you must" and went over and took the little apparition out of the window, with an air of distaste as if she was handling something unsavoury. She stood it up on the counter and looked at it with extreme disapproval.

"This is the last one we have of these, thankfully. They were made by a local craftsman as a memento of the awful story attached to the Old House, as a town souvenir, but we stopped selling them because people were complaining, they are just too gruesome, and the trustees of the Old House were complaining, it was just too over the top. So once this goes, we won't be getting in anymore. Though some people with a warped sense of humour used to quite take to them. They're actually 'collectible'" She surveyed the little doll and miniature gallows with a sour look. "I personally think some people must be really warped."

But Jenny picked it up and dangled it in front of her eyes, enthralled.

"So this is Evelyn?"

The shop owner turned up one side of her top lip slightly. "Yes, that is the infamous Evelyn Hardy".

But Jenny was enervated. "It looks just like her! Look, it's got exactly the same figure, the dress is identical, and even her little face...."

"Well, the doll-maker copied from that photograph of her in foyer of the Old House, and that dress they have in the glass case in the museum".

Jenny turned round beamed at Chris, her mind made up. "Let's buy it!"

Chris recoiled in horror and shook his head.

"No, no, I don't want that in the house., It's too gruesome. It's sick. It's perverted. I've had enough of that place. Put it back. You know how she scared Bobby. Do you think we want that thing in the house on display, someone dangling on the end of a rope? What would people think when we come to visit us? Buy something else, a picture, a plate, a tea towel, an ashtray, a teaspoon, anything, but I don't want that in the house!".

Jenny put it back down despondently, said "Thanks" to the owner, and they walked out.

After they had gone, the shop assistant picked it up, looked at it for some seconds with the same look of distaste as before, and then as if finally making a decision dropped it in the waste basket under the counter.

Chris and Jenny walked along silently for some minutes, then suddenly Jenny saw something on the other side of the road and screamed.

"Look!!" She pointed. "There's Evelyn!!"

Standing on the footpath on the other side of the road by a vacant lot was what looked like the guide who had shown through the house, scratching herself and looking up and down the street, with her feet pointing outwards in her characteristic pose.

Jenny screamed out to her 'Evelyn!'".

The woman heard, and stood frozen for a second, looking at Jenny. Then Jenny put Bobby's hand in the hand of Chris, roughly handed him her shoulder bag, and rushed across the road towards the blue-clad figure, almost getting run over by a car. But as soon as Jenny started towards her, the woman picked up her skirts so she wouldn't trip and turned and scuttled like a frightened rabbit across the vacant lot, then clambered over a fence at the back of it that was about as high as her. When she scaled it, she did it by clumsily throwing herself at it, then lifting one leg up so her boot was hooked over the top of it, and somehow squirmed herself over it. But when Jenny reached the fence, even though there was clear land at the back of it as far as the eye could see, Evelyn, if that was her, was nowhere to be seen.

Chris, leading Bobby by the hand, finally joined Jenny at the fence.

"That was her! That was her! That was our guide" screamed Jenny. "That was Evelyn!"

"It was too far away to tell for sure" said Chris, rather irritably, as if he was getting bored with the whole thing. "It must have been that looney woman the girl at the desk was telling us about".

"Well then where is she? She couldn't have got far enough away to be out of sight in that space of time. I got to this fence in about ten seconds!"

Chris shrugged, getting more and more impatient with the whole affair.

"Maybe she disappeared down a rabbit-hole, I don't know!"

Jenny turned away from the fence and started walking back to the street. She took Bobby's hand from Chris and her shoulder bag.

"Rabbit holes!" she said derisively. "Yes, she looked like she could fit down a rabbit hole! Secret passages into the house. Coming down the chimney! Coming in through locked windows. We've seen a ghost, that's what we've seen! We've been given a guided tour by a ghost. And we've just seen her again.

"Did you notice no-one was looking at her when she ran across the vacant lot, but they looked at me. Maybe we were the only ones who could see her!"

They walked on towards where their car was parked.

"No, you know what I think?" said Chris after neither had spoken for some time.

"It's that looney girl. She gave us the tour, and we just saw her again. Do you know there's such a thing as an idiot savant?"

"That's another big word for you!"

"It's a French term that means someone incredibly stupid, but incredibly clever in some areas as well. It's one particular kind of mental aberration".

"Well that's not you, for a start, you're just incredibly stupid".

He ignored the remark. "They can have photographic memories, and an incredible ability to memorise long passages, she could have memorised that whole spiel about the history of the house. And they can be incredibly inventive and can see solutions to things other people can't. Maybe she worked out a way to get in and out of the house without being seen.

"And all that fake business like pretending she didn't know what a modern camera looked like, pretending she didn't know what 'to take pictures' meant, talking about walking round with a candle, saying 'The horses must be tired', .. it was all a very clever bit of play-acting."

'But what about the key to the attic?"

"That, I can't explain. But just because I can't explain everything.....

"Anyway. We're never going back, and you're not taking Bobby there again! The poor kid was traumatised."

Jenny looked very thoughtful for a while, and a bit disappointed at having her balloon pricked. Then she said thoughtfully.:

"So either we saw a ghost, or that looney woman isn't as looney as people think, and she can sneak in there somehow, and take that dress out of the locked glass case and put it on, and get out without being seen, or fake a dress to look like it's 100 years old, and knows every little anecdote about the history of the family and the house and every little nook and cranny of the house even though no-one 's ever told her and grunts and abuses people all the time except when she's within these four walls when she suddenly become personable and eloquent, and she can flit around the rooms like a moth, now you see her, now you don't... ...." Jenny had calmed down and was no longer combative about the whole affair and was talking half to herself and half to Chris.

"We just don't know....."

They walked on slowly for a few more minutes, each holding one of Bobby's hands, and Chris said

"We'll never know......"

THE SWITCHEROO

or
take your fantasies for reality

It was his favourite show. Every Thursday night he would rush home to be sure to be there at 9.30 and not miss the beginning. He was angry with himself if he ever missed even the first few minutes. It was something to look forward to for the rest of the week, which, he sometimes reflected, might be a sad comment on the emptiness of his life.

Be that as it may. this weekly escape into fantasy had ensnared his imagination, for better or for worse...

The show was called "Haden at Large" and the hero was one Irving Haden, a freelance spy-cum-private-investigator-cum-soldier-of-fortune, who every week was dispatched to one of the four corners of the world on some fantastic caper, which was guaranteed to involve at least two women of unsurpassable beauty, one car chase, three shoot-outs, (sometimes a beautiful woman, a car chase and a shoot out all at once) and a fist-fight whose gymnastics and choreography would make a professional wrestling match look tame in comparison.

Irving Haden had dark, thick hair, with just a hint of a wave in it, and one heavy lock that always hung boyishly over one side of his forehead no matter how many times he flicked it back. He had clean-cut, regular features, and whether he was cracking a joke, whether he was in peril of his life in a shoot-out or a car chase with a mob of desperados, there was always a cheeky, roguish grin playing about his lips, so that you never knew whether to take him seriously. He had a way of looking at people askance, slightly narrowing his eyes, cocking one eyebrow, and giving them that ambiguous smile, so that they were never sure what was to come next. The girls loved him. He could always come out with that smart crack at the right time - they always melted under his charm, not like those stand-offish, bitchy, cantankerous, smug, contrary females in the real world.

Everything Haden did was slick, neat, down to every little movement he made. John Clarke was sure that, deep down inside, he himself was like that. If ever he had the chance to be in any of the situations such as happened in the show, he was sure he would shine, he was sure he would rise heroically to the occasion. But how could he ever prove what he was made of, when his whole existence was ground into the business of being a ... wait for it......bank clerk! Yaarggh! What a difference!

Do you know what his job entailed? He sat at a desk all day, and at that desk various weird and wonderful documents came, were acted on by him, and were sent on. He could recite his duties like a catechism. Each form had a number. The 401B's went to Harold Lisle in head office. The 409s had to be matched with a 50B and sent to Arthur Phillips on the fourth floor, unless they didn't have a yellow copy, in which case they were stamped and sent to Kevin Rigby. Then at the end of the day he had to do his daily summary, and at the end of the week he did his weekly summary, and at the end of his month he did his monthly summary. How insufferably boring! His whole existence was dedicated to make one big account of money, the assets of the bank, grow bigger and bigger!

At the end of his life, what would they say? Here lies John Clarke. What did he do? Answer: He filled in some forms ...

The manager had come up to him at the end of his first month at the job. He said "You're fitting in well here, Clarke".

Fitting in well? Or in other words, he had been trimmed and honed and dressed and every bit of him that was himself had been chopped off so he would slide neatly into one little pre-arranged hole, Like a tree that is trimmed down until there's nothing left of it but a tent-peg, he had been processed into something that was no longer human. Like a galley slave chained to the oar, he existed for no other purpose than to drive the faceless, boring organization, The Bank, forward.

"It's so pleasing" the same manager had said at his after dinner speech at the last Christmas party "to see these fine young people, becoming part of our team, being absorbed into the industry...."

Absorbed into the industry! What was he? A droplet on the great sponge of human existence, with no other destiny than to be intermingled? He didn't want to be absorbed! He didn't want to fit in! He'd rather be a misfit that had to be thrown out of the great machine because he was indigestible to it! At least he would retain his own self. He didn't want to be "part of a team!"

But he forgot all that when he was watching "Haden at Large".

Sometimes, annoyingly, he would get a phone call in the middle of the show. Happily the phone was right by his chair so he could talk and watch at the same time. If it was someone he couldn't get rid of quickly, he would only say "yeah...yeah...mmm.... mmm that's right...did you? ....really....." without listening to what was being said to him, his eyes glued to the screen. Sometimes he even took the phone off the hook so his watching should not be interrupted.

Was this unhealthy? Was fantasy destructive? He asked himself often this question. Was it unhealthy to harbour impossible dreams inside yourself? He liked to think it wasn't, but something told him it was. After much conjecture he had formulated a theory that people fantasised every moment of their lives. When you were hungry, you fantasised about having something to eat, then you had something to eat. When you were tired you fantasised about how good it would be to rest, so you rested. Everything that happened to you, on the large plane, or on the trivial plane, could be reduced to fantasy and fulfilment, or fantasy and frustration. The vision was the necessary precursor to the reality. Therefore fantasy could be healthy, because it formulated your goal, in order that that goal could be achieved. Then who could dismiss any fantasy as impossible? There were people who lived the life Irving Haden lived. Maybe he could be one of them.....Besides, wasn't everyone who indulged themselves in the idiot box, or lost themselves in a book, fantasising? When you were moved to emotion by a fictional drama, your emotion was identical to what it would be if it were really happening.

So, at the age of 22, having just enough money to rent himself a dingy apartment, drive a passable car, and provide the basic luxuries of life, here was John Clarke. At the stage of his life when, it seemed to him, he was bursting at the seams with energy, with potential, with ideas, with visions of what could be, he found himself constricted, shackled and strait-jacketed into a routine that took only one thousandth part of what abilities he was endowed with, and only satisfied an equal part of his zest for life. All in all, his world was a world of banality, of the commonplace, of intellectual squalor. His world was like a prison, and the television screen when "Haden At Large" was on was a window through which he could see out of the prison.

It was three quarters of an hour into the show, and Irving Haden had just been visited in his swanky apartment by a shamelessly unpleasant villain who had threatened to do him in, in an especially vile and barbaric way, if Haden did not get off the trail of the criminal gang he was intent on pursuing and bringing to justice. Haden had handled the confrontation with his usual tongue-in-cheek coolness, treating it as if it were a joke, as if it was a little game they were playing, that had no more importance than sparring for places in a game of snakes and ladders, and was not a matter of life and death – in fact, his life and his death. This, of course, had infuriated the villain no end, and he had departed in a rage. Despite his insouciance, it looked grim for Haden. How would he get out of this one? But then, it always looked that way about this far through the show, and he always won through. You always knew he would. Now he was pacing the floor, drawing on a cigarette, as if planning his next move. Then suddenly, he turned and looked straight at the camera. He said

"Hey buddy, you wanna swap places with me?"

John Clarke was confused. He thought he had been following the plot closely, but now he could not understand to whom Haden was supposed to be talking. He had thought there was no-one else in the room. Irving Haden still looked straight out of the screen.

His voice became impatient at not being answered. "I said, 'Would you like to swap places with me?'"

His eyes seemed to be fixed on John Clarke, and that playful, mock-serious, completely inpenetratable smile was on his lips.

"Hey, buddy. I'm talking to you!"

It was eerie. It did indeed seem as if the character was talking to him. Who was he meant to be talking to? It was not clear. It seemed like an oversight by the scriptwriter, to leave out the entrance into the room of the hero's interlocutor. And what did he mean "swap places with him"?

"John Clarke!"

John Clarke, sitting in his soft armchair, in the privacy of his lounge room, started.

"That's you, isn't it? John Clarke?"

The hero's voice had taken on a slightly impatient tone.

"Hey, buddy, I'm talking to you!"

John Clarke sat up in his chair, looked left and right, and behind him. What was going on? Why was Irving Haden calling out his name. His name! Could there be someone in the script with the same name as him? How weird! He got up and leapt to the door and opening it quickly, looked out into the hallway, as if, absurdly, he hoped to find the answer to the mystery there. When he saw the hallway was empty, he returned and looked at the television again. Irving Haden still had his eyes fixed demandingly on him, and seemed to look so real, he seemed to be there in the living room, as if the television screen was just a window he was looking through.

Now Haden frowned in impatience. "You are John Clarke, aren't you?"

John Clarke ran round the back of the set, as if he expected to find the answer to the mystery there, as if he expected to find Haden kneeling down there with his head poking through the back of the set. But of course, the set looked no different at the back to what he would have expected. Then he thought someone had played a practical joke on him, and had contrived to record a video, with someone impersonating the great star, and now addressing him by his name. Absurd as this proposition was, it was the only wild theory that came anywhere near to fitting the facts, but he saw the video machine was not even plugged in.

He returned to the front of the set. Haden still had his eyes fixed on him. John Clarke tried to change channels, but whatever channel he turned to, the picture on the screen stayed the same. Irving Haden's eyes seemed to be looking down into the corner of the screen with a frown, watching him. Then he tried to turn the set off, but there seemed to be something wrong with the switch, for the switch would not turn off, and the picture would not go away.

"Would you like to swap places with me?" again demand Irving Haden.

He found himself saying "Well.....yes!"

Haden nodded, as if it was just as he had expected.

"You watch me every week, don't you?"

"Why...yes!"

"You must be my greatest fan". He fixed on John Clarke a warm, appreciative, ingratiating smile.

"So, how'd you like to swap places with me?"

It was said in that tantalising, encouraging wey, that you know is going to suck you in, when something you awant is waved justunder your nose, even though you know there must be a catch to it.

"What? You mean....I do what you do, and you take over what I do? Well...." John Clarke was at a loss to know what to answer for a moment, then, realised there was only one thing he could say that would not stultify every wish, every fantasy, every empathetic move he had made in the last three months of following the show.

"Yes! Of course I would."

Haden then started walking round his room, dragging heavily on the cigarette, as if he was debating something inwardly.

"What do you do?"

"I'm a bank clerk".

Haden shrugged. "Sounds good. What hours do you work?"

John Clarke frowned, as if it was an obvious question. "Start at nine, finish at five"

"Sounds good. What do you do after you finish work?"

John Clarke shrugged, as if it that also were a strange question. "Why, whatever I want to do".

"You mean once you leave work, you can do as you like?"

"Yes"

"Anybody gunning for you?"

"No".

"Have to check your car every morning to see it hasn't been booby-trapped?"

"No!"

"Ever been cracked over the head with a pistol butt?"

"No".

"Ever had to jump from a first floor window to save your life and landed on concrete, or in thorn-bushes?"

"No!"

"How much vacation do you get?"

"Four weeks a year"

"And you go where you like, do what you like?"

"Of course"

"Sounds good."

"But...why on earth would you want to change with me? Your life is so exciting, so adventurous..."

"Ahhh, I'm getting sick of it. I tear all round the world, I risk my neck every day, I get shot at, mugged, threatened, jumped on, escape with my life by the skin of my teeth three times every week..... I want to lead a normal life. I want to come home, put my feet up, read a newspaper, relax, drink a beer....." He sounded genuinely frustrated, genuinely eager to give away the grandeur.

"But the adventure.....!".

"Ahhhh who needs adventure? You know what adventure really is? Not knowing if you're going to be dead or alive five minutes from now. It's like sky diving, or playing Russian Roulette.. The thrill is proportionate to the risk of 'getting it'. Well, I don't intend to 'get it'. I want to live! Being a bank clerk sounds great"

"But why me, to swap places with, of all people?"

Haden fixed on him that penetrating, overwhelming smile, and pointed a compelling finger towards John Clarke.

"Because you're good, pal, you're really good. I've been watching you, and asking some questions about you, and I've found that you're…." he made a clicking sound with his teeth, as if he was lost for superlatives and that would have to suffice "you're good. You've got what it takes. You're wasted out there. This is where you belong".

He had that presence that made the most banal, transparent, plausible kind of buttering up, stick like gold leaf.

John Clarke stood before the set, transfixed. He didn't know what to say.

"So… if you think you'd like that kind of life…. why don't you just, step on through".

At this moment, his hand came right out of the television screen, extended to John Clarke, who felt an irresistible urge to put his own hand forward to meet it, it looked so real. He expected to ultimately come up against the glass of the TV screen, but to his shock, it seemed to pass right through, and he found himself holding the live hand of Irving Haden. The screen had become an open window into the world he had made his fantasy, a window he could reach through.

Haden's hand had a warm, strong, compelling grip.

"Just - step on through!"

It was like one of those ridiculous quiz shows. "Step on down!".

He found himself lifting one leg, and putting it into the screen that had become a window and into the inside of the set, but, no resistance met it, and easing his whole body through, with some help form the brawny arms of Irving Haden he found himself climbing out into the apartment he had so often seen in the show. Then he was right the way through, and standing up on his feet, having come out through the television in the apartment. Now, on the screen of this television set in Irving Haden's apartment, he could see his own poky flat, as if it was being filmed. Haden beamed at him in welcome.

"How d'you like it?"

He looked around. It was five times as big as his own. He stepped across to the window and looked out. From a great height, he was seeing the pulsating, brilliant night landscape of New York.

"We're on the twenty-fifth floor! That's New York city down there! Here…."

He unstrapped his shoulder holster, lifted John Clarke's jacket, and strapped it onto him. He took the gun out, and placed it meaningfully in John Clarke's hand, as if it were a trophy.

It was the first time he had even held a gun. It was heavier than he expected, but it felt good. It was cold, real. He squeezed it. It made him feel strong, secure, dangerous. He pointed it playfully at Haden for no apparent reason, and pretended to take aim, but Haden pushed his arm away with an instinctive movement. "Hey, man! Watch it. That thing's loaded!"

John Clarke looked down at the gun in his hand in amazement.

"You mean, It can actually shoot?"

Haden looked uncomprehending for a moment. "Of course. What use is a gun that can't shoot? But hey, you hold it well. It was made for you".

John Clarke felt proud. He turned his wrist slightly back and forth, savouring the feel of the gun. It sure did feel good.

He looked around the apartment. He eyes fell on the framed photo of a stunning woman, lying half prone on a beach, resting on her arms behind her, and her chest thrust up into the air, as if in a celebration of voluptuousness, of life. From her dazzling white teeth, her scarlet lips, her hair, her flawless skin, her perfectly shaped body, she looked like one of those girls who exude enjoyment, pleasure from every pore. It was like a posed shot from a girlie magazine, it was designed to excite you and entice you, but this wasn't from a magazine, it was a personal photograph, and signed "For you, baby!"

Haden read his thoughts and looked John Clarke right in the eye, intently.

"That's Ingrid! Wow, is she put together, eh? You'll be seeing her tonight. She's coming round to take you out, to welcome you back to town!"

"SHE's coming round to take ME out?" squealed John Clarke in disbelief.

"Sure thing! She's wants to make the most of the one night she's got you. You're flying off to Europe on an assignment tomorrow, with Anne-Louise."

"Anne-Louise!"

He couldn't follow it all. He felt dizzy trying to.

He felt as if someone were holding an intoxicating drug under his nose, and he was floating away on the irresistible scent.

Haden waved his hand towards the picture of another girl, which was hung on the wall. "And that's Samantha, Sammy, the pilot, when she's not modelling, or making movies, or skiing. Owns her own executive jet. Likes to wing you off to faraway places whenever she can get hold of you! He slapped him encouragingly on the shoulder. "Hey! I think you're going to be a big hit with all these girls!"

Now John Clarke saw Irving Haden in close up, he looked different, and much older than he had seen him as on the set. He had thought he was about 35, or younger. Now, he looked like he was in his early fifties, maybe even older. His hair was such a perfect consistency of jet black, he knew it must be dyed. He was wearing make-up, to make himself look tanned. He was sure he had false teeth, and not only that, he could see the contact lenses in his eyes. Even the expression on his face looked different, now you saw him in real life. He looked no longer cocky, cheeky, adventuresome, he looked like someone with something to sell. That was it: he looked like nothing more or less than a salesman. He looked brazen, pushy, as if he were intent on cajoling you into something against your will.

Haden took a keycase from his pocket, and held the keys up individually enunciating the purpose of each one.

"The Maserati….the Jag…the Mustang…Samantha's place……Samantha's plane. Ingrid's place…… Ingrid's car…..the key to this place…" Then he presented the set to John Clarke ceremoniously, and held out his hand as if for something in return.

"You got the keys to your place? The keys of your car?"

John Clarke fumbled nervously in his pocket for them, and gave them to Haden. "Which is the car?" demanded Haden, as if it were an important point. John Clarke showed him.

"What is it?"

"Toyota Corona" said John Clarke apologetically.

"Yeah? One of those economical, Japanese four cylinder jobs, eh? Sounds good. Man, I hate trying to park those tanks in New York". He seemed to be genuinely pleased.

He made a grandiose gesture with his arm, indicating the apartment. "Well, this is all yours, now, pal!" Then he took a meaningful, portentous step back.

"Well, must hit the trail, pal".

He lifted one leg and placed it through the television screen, just as John Clarke had done, and lifted himself through to the modest flat where John Clarke had had his abode. John Clarke could see him, walking round, examining his humble new home, evidently with approval.

Suddenly there was a tremendous thumping on the door of Haden's, that was now John Clarke's, apartment.

"Hey, Haden! You in there? We've come for you, buddy! You're going to get yours!"

John Clarke looked through the screen at Irving Haden helplessly, his arms waving in despair at his side.

"What should I do?"

Haden spoke deliberately and without hesitation, with that commanding presence John Clarke had come to expect.

"Point the gun right at the centre of the door, hold it with both hands, and shoot!"

John Clarke had never fired a gun. He did as he was told, his arms shaking so much he could hardly take aim. He winced, turned his head to one side as he pulled the trigger, as if he was afraid the gun might explode. The noise of the gunshot in the apartment was deafening. Immediately he heard a gutteral cry of anguish. Evidently they had not been prepared for that. John Clarke looked transfixed at the jagged hole in the door he had just been responsible for. He had actually shot someone. Maybe killed someone. And he didn't even know who it was. What had he become? What kind of world had he stepped into?

"Keep shooting! Keep shooting! Give'em the works! It's the only chance you've got!"

John Clarke did as he was told. What did he mean? 'it's the only chance you've got". There was an obvious question he wanted to ask Haden but he was so scared for his life he pumped four more rounds through the door before he spoke.

"Hey! These are real bullets!" he screamed to Irving Haden.

Haden held his hands palms upward in a gesture of "What did you expect? "I told you. This is the real thing, man. It's what you wanted!"

No more groans came from behind the door. Of course not. Why would they? They would have stepped out of the way after that first shot. He was just wasting bullets. Nevertheless he kept firing to keep them from coming back to the door. Then, one more shot, and the gun just clicked.

He could not believe it. The gun had suddenly become his protector, his salvation, the only thing between him and death, and he could not believe it would ever fail him, it was supposed to be a bottomless well of strength.

Then, with the lull in his firing, he heard more sounds behind the door. They had guessed his gun was empty, and had come back. There was a deafening explosion from outside, and simultaneously, he saw a gaping hole appear in the door, and heard a bullet hit something behind him. He looked through the screen of the television set at Haden in horror.

"I do not like this! I do not like this one bit!" he declaimed. "I hope the next episode is more fun than this. Just tell me how I'm supposed to escape from these bastards! I'm out of bullets, and I'm on the 25th floor, and they're between me and the lift! What have you got? A helicopter outside? What about that sheila that flies planes. Couldn't she be out there hovering in a chopper and lift me clear." Now he thought of it, he remembered just such a sequence from a previous episode.

Haden lifted his chin, and his face glowed with cocky triumph, as if he had just put over on someone

one heck of an enormous joke. "I got news for you, buddy. Make the most of this. This is going to be your one taste of adventure. This is going to be your one taste of the fast life. In fact, this is going to be your last taste of life! Why do you think I wanted out? There ain't going to be no more episodes! This is the last Mohican. They're scrapping the series. And to make sure no-one asks them to bring it back, they're killing me, sorry, I mean YOU off- Tonight! That was why the old switcheroo You die, and I live. You wanted adventure, pal! You got it! But me, I'm going to step right in to a cushy, comfortable easy job for the rest of my life! So - so long, sucker!"

Haden threw is head back and laughed uproariously. John Clarke rushed to the set to climb back through, but when he touched the screen it was solid. He pounded it with his hand, but it was as cold and inpenetratable as a TV screen should be. Only the cruel, mocking, victorious face of Irving Haden laughing hysterically looked back at him. He heard another shot, and felt a great impact, and a tearing pain in his right arm. The door burst open and three individuals of unimaginably evil aspect, including the one who had threatened Irving Haden earlier, charged through like bulls coming through a gate. He pointed his gun in desperation again with his left arm and pulled the trigger, but it just clicked.

The three grinned maliciously, and, in unison, raised their guns slowly towards him, holding their weapons at arms length, with both hands, as if, even at that short distance, their hatred for him was so great they were determined not to miss. He wished for anything to be back in his own world, in his own home, sitting in comfort in his own familiar armchair, watching this happening to someone else, knowing that in a few minutes he could turn it off, and retire to a peaceful, safe bed.

As he waited for the blast, which, in a black horror that was so great he could not have described it, he knew would mean his death, the end, all for the sake of a few moments of excitement, of his short life, the words of Irving Haden echoed in his ears..... "So long...so long...you SUCKER!"

A NOBLE BATTLE

Two armies lay on opposite sides of a great moor, licking their wounds, recuperating and calculating their next move. Temporarily the inclement weather had put a cessation to the slaughter, for visibility through the mist was much less than the distance of an arrow-flight. The drizzle had soaked the ground so much that it was a brave and skilled rider who could raise anything more than a stumbling walk on even the driest sections of the plain. So time had graciously allowed the two foes to bind their wounds, to bury their dead and plot their next moves.

One army was clad in black, the other white, an accident of history that seemed to have an ironic significance, as if the two sides were so akin to one another, if they were not adorned like this they would have massacred their own kind, or given up fighting

Behind the frontline of the white forces some foot soldiers were talking around a camp fire. One declaimed "Who is it who are first into battle? It is us. Who is it who suffer the first losses? It is us. Who is it who bear the greatest share of the onslaught from the charge of the enemy, who are where the arrows are thickest, who have no horses on which to flee when the situation is hopeless? It is we - the infantry. We are nothing! We are just fodder. We are moved about at will from here to here, and if we fall that a knight may live, it is regarded as a cheap sacrifice. Our value is at inverse proportion to our numbers. There are more of us, therefore each one of us is worth less."

He had spoken without a pause, as if he had carried his thoughts inside himself for as long as he had been a foot-soldier, and they had matured like wine while he contemplated his lot through the long, lonely nights of war. He was bitter, and he was sure of his ideas. Though some thought his words unreasonable, none contradicted him, he was too full of passion.

"I feel sometimes an unseen hand moves us" joined in another "and it is not in our hands that our fate lies, or even in the hands of the king. We will win, or they will win - who can say? We came into this world - born without our asking into a certain kingdom, in a certain time, let us say - moulded into a certain colour, and condemned for ever, as if as a punishment for our existence, to fight under that colour's banners. There are no rights or wrongs to it. It is destiny - the power bigger than ourselves and unknown to ourselves picks us up, knocks us down, scatters us. Fate moves us".

He withdrew his sword from his scabbard and drew a line with it in the mud, then significantly indicated a mark first one side of it, and then the other.

"Think" he explained. "If the line that marks the division between the two kingdoms was 20 miles to the west, I would be fighting for the enemy, I would be trying to kill you. I would be doing it for their glory instead of ours.

"And who are this "enemy" we must fight? Are they so bad? Are they born with some moral deformity that condemns them to suffer whatever we do to them? We are taught history from our point of view. No doubt whatever would bring discredit on us has been purged from the pages of our chronicles, and many heroic acts that would bring admiration onto the heads of our enemies have passed into obscurity. So why do we fight? We fight for nothing more than selfishness, that we might have everything and they might have nothing.

"Yes, we must fight, for it would be dishonourable to surrender our territory without fighting for it, even if we are doomed to lose it. But then, what is honourable, or dishonourable? We only call this territory "ours" because our ancestors conquered it from another tribe. How many lives equal the value of drawing a line on the map? And yet, even as I speak, I feel it can be no other way. How strange! War is the natural state of our race. I feel we would not exist if we had no-one to make war with. It is the definition of what we are. If we had no enemy to fight, we would fight each other. If we could not fight ourselves we would make war on our own shadows. Life is black and white, we need the two opposites to make the whole- night and day, man and woman, land and sea.

"It is a role we are born to play, a ridiculous, choreographed play-acting. We are moved out of the forest to a certain hill. There we find we are to draw the enemies' fire, and many of us are lost. So why were we on the hill? As a sacrifice to draw the fire so that some knight could skip past them. Would we have placed ourselves there of our own volition? No. We are moved about as if we have no value but are insignificant parts in a stage-play. Perhaps I don't mean only this battle, but life itself...if we have been cast white we must fight the black, if were cast black we fight the white, it is our sorry lot, until the long game's over and we are....well, what?...thrown back in the box, let us say. That is how it seems to me".

Meanwhile at the ancestral seat of the royal court, in the castle where resided the embattled king of the black forces and his queen there was no joy. Never had morale in all the four years of the war been so low. It was winter. The sun had not been seen for weeks. A continual drizzle of icy rain afflicted the whole countryside. Bleak mists wafted in pockets across the valley. Everything was damp and chill to the touch. That chill seemed to match the chill in their souls, the gloom seemed to match the gloom in their hearts when they contemplated how much had been lost to the enemy.

Three fourths of the kingdom was in white hands. Villages where a year ago the king had ridden triumphant were now occupied by the white soldiers. Only the inhospitable nature of the marshy, wild country, had temporarily halted the ineluctable approach of defeat.

In the great hall of the castle sat five figures. An artist with an eye for shape and form might have noticed a piquant elegance in the arrangement of the forlorn group, for they formed the extremities of a triangulated prism, as though they were posed for a painting. The king sat on his throne, his head sunk on his hand. The queen was on the third step below, her long blond hair being plaited by a pale, thin-faced, demure maid-in-waiting. A sturdy, heavily-armoured figure was to her right, whose upright bearing and formidable appearance betokened him to be a knight. The group was completed by an old, portly figure, clad in the plain, humble vestments of a holy man. This was the grand old bishop of the established church of the kingdom. On all matters pertaining to the fortunes of the kingdom he had the ear of the king. They called him the "King's Bishop". He had served three generations of the ruling house and seen plague, war, victory, humiliation, pestilence, years of plenty and years of drought. He had seen royal births, royal deaths, intrigue of brother against brother, uncle against nephew and survived it all. It was thought this had given him wisdom unsurpassed.

Now he faced the King and said:

"There is but one thing can save us, your majesty. I can ride to the other castle and get help."

"But you are an old man" said the King. "You are not even a horseman. You cannot dodge and dart this way and that on the battlefield like our knights."

"Your majesty, I have a dependable horse, and despite my size I can move far and fast in a straight line. I will not go the way of the Knights, where the battle rages. I will cut across the plain, then turn and head straight for the furthermost shores where our other castle is. Because I am a man of the cloth I will be guaranteed safe passage through hostile vil-lages. I can rally our forces there, and bring them to our aid. Meanwhile, you and the queen must stay near the castle, but keep on the move, dodging the enemy, until I return. Your last loyal knight will stay with you.

"Your majesty, it is our only chance. A foot soldier went out this morning to scout and did not return. His death told us eloquently that the enemy are closing in."

The king still appearing uncertain, the bishop played his trump-card.

"Your majesty - you can spare no-one else".

For two minutes no sound could be heard but the dripping of the rain and the wailing of the wind. Not a muscle of the king's face moved to betray his thoughts, but all knew what he was thinking. He was reflecting sadly the state his country had come to that it must send old, feeble men, such a fat, comical figure, a man of the cloth, on such a desperate errand.

"All right. Go" said the king at last.

The bishop drew his cloak around him and waddled into the rain. They heard his petulant voice arguing with his poor old mare as he dragged his rotund form onto her back. Then they heard the beast's unsteady steps receding into the darkness.

Sunrise over the forlorn landscape brought only news of defeat after defeat for the black-clad forces. They found themselves trapped in positions on the battlefield where it appeared the enemy had foreseen they would be, and so were decimated, few escaping capture or death. It was as though the tactics of those who decreed their movements had been based on erroneous judgments of the enemy's next move. However, it had been so since the start of the war, strategies had continually been more important than numbers, in fact at the start numerically they had been evenly matched. Now, however, as their numbers decreased, the growing advantage of numbers became preponderant - detached groups found themselves surrounded, and with no safe place to move, and where reinforcements had been before, there were only gaps in their ranks.

When night fell again and the absence of a moon brought a longed for lull to the advance of the white hordes, a large party of the black wounded found themselves encamped for shelter beneath the walls of the castle. They were the most severely wounded who could take no further part in the war. The king, the queen, and the king's most loyal knight, came down and walked among them, dispensing royal commiserations. What could be said, however, that was not so many hollow words to be blown away by the wind, when the only question in the soldiers' minds was: which would come first, their deaths, or the arrival of the enemy?

The king gripped the hand of a sinewy old warrior. The soldier, his face showing he was tired of pain and tired of the war, stared glumly up at his monarch.

"I tell you, my man" said the king "We are not beaten. You will live to walk among the enemy as a conqueror, and...."

He was cut off in the middle of a sentence, for a heavy, bedraggled figure towing a limping horse appeared out of the mist. There was no mistaking that waddling gait and portly shape. The king addressed it.

"Good Bishop. We had given you up for dead. Tell us! Have you brought our soldiers from our other castle? Are we saved? Is the tide of the battle to turn? How is the other castle standing up to the enemy?"

The Bishop, his black cloak torn to shreds, his face besmirched with the dirt of the roads, the corners of his fat lips turned down in a pathetic mask of extreme despair, could not look his monarch in the eye. He stared straight ahead past the king into the night.

"Your majesty, I have to tell you the other castle has fallen. I bring no aid. I was pursued by the enemy. I only lost them because I could find my way in the dark through the marshes and they could not. Why, even now I may have been pursued. I...."

At that instant an arrow caught him in the back, he gave a deep groan and fell at the king's feet. The queen screamed in horror. The enemy king, flanked by two young knights, and four foot - soldiers appeared with a clatter of armour, like spectres out of the night.

The queen knew it was the end, but she grabbed the king's sword and, rushing forward, ran though the nearest white knight who, caught by the shock of so sudden an onslaught, had no time to retaliate and fell off his horse, dead. But it was a doomed victory. At the end of her headlong rush a foot soldier simply stepped in her path and cut her down. The king moved a few steps to be with his beloved, but was confronted by the other knight. He tried to move this way and that. Although no attempt was made to strike him, whichever way he moved his path was blocked, and he was unarmed. It was truly the end.

"Checkmate! I think".

In the dim room lit only by the flickering fire, the air thick with tobacco smoke from the old man's pipe, the two players could hardly see each other. The lateness, the somnolent, slow, ticking of the grandfather clock, the fine, old, rich, dark, oaky taste of the port, formed an ambiance conducive to only sleepiness, reverie and philosophical reflection. Although these words marked the end of the game, the result seemed to be now a detached event, happening to someone else, which they could look at from a distance.

The old man picked up the black king, and held it up in his hand. It was a handsome piece, about four inches high, and intricately carved out of some wood so fine-grained it could take the most painstakingly fine detail of the carver's art.

"It's a beautiful set, don't you think?" he said to his opponent. "Take this king - the face, why, it's carved so delicately, you can see the expression on it. It's got a personality all its own. Hmmmph!. Just looking at him now, he doesn't look too happy. Look at the emotion carved into that face. It actually looks like the monarch of a kingdom who's just lost a battle, lost his queen, lost his land, lost his sovereignty, lost everything. Just look at the expression on that face".

He held it for his opponent to see.

"It's almost as if he were real!"

MERLIN IN HIS CAVE

A knight dismounted his horse outside the mouth of a cave. He was huge and covered from head to foot in chain mail and solid armour. He had a gigantic sword in a scabbard hanging from his waist that looked as if it would take two men to lift it, leave alone swing it. His face was bearded, gnarled and foreboding, he almost looked more like a gorilla than a man.

He had two other knights with him who by their demeanor were clearly underlings to his authority. They dismounted when he dismounted, and were obviously watching him to see where they should proceed next.

It was the 'Year of Our Lord" 541.

"Old man, old man!" the head knight shouted into the cave. "Come out, old man. I have words to speak with you!" His loud voice echoed among the rocks.

Faint footsteps could be heard in the depths of the cave, faint footsteps that got louder. Eventually an old, slightly built, sinewy man but with an alert face and bright eyes appeared. He seemed pleased to see his visitors, though he did not know their purpose.

He held out his thin hand to the knight and beamed while he said "I am Merlin!"

The knight ignored his hand, but declared in stentorian tones. "Old man! It has been said you are engaged in the work of the devil, and are calling up evil spirits that endanger our kingdom, It is said you are building machines and weapons and concocting potions that could be used by our enemies. I am here as an emissary of the king to see for myself what you are about!"

This was true. It was rumoured the old man was invoking the forces of darkness to do unnatural things that had no explanation. He had been aa a young boy a brilliant student, mastering languages, arithmetic, geometry, history, and a knowledge of the scriptures, all areas of learning, before others many years his senior. He both exasperated and enthralled his teachers - exasperated because he was forever arguing with them, telling them things they said were not possible were possible, and continually asking "why?", and enthralling them with his capacity to absorb knowledge. When he corrected a teacher on some point, always he was found to be right and the teacher wrong.

He had been apprenticed to several trades, but had become bored with each, and always ended up being dismissed by his masters for spending too much time experimenting with better ways of doing things.

So he had become a recluse, eking a living by repairing carts, musical instruments, toys, weaponry… any moving implement that was broken. It was seldom a damaged item was beyond his ability to repair. Usually it was returned not only fixed but much improved because of some alteration Merlin had made to it.

But questions began to be asked when he brought dying farm animals back to life with potions he concocted, and when he made fantastic claims that one day there would be no need of horses to pull carts, or sails to move ships, and mankind would be free of many diseases due to experiments he was conducting in his cave. Such a man, it was said, must have made a pact with the devil.

He now held out his hands in front of himself with palms upward in a gesture of peace, then grabbed the right hand of the knight in both his hands and shook it with relish. "Call me Merlin!" he said. "That is my name. Work of the devil? Why, it is just the opposite! This is the work that will smite the devil, give us victory over all the ills of the land! With my inventions we will conquer all the dark forces of the world! We will have …"

"Enough" replied the knight impatiently, pushing Merlin away. "Show me what evil contrivances you have in the recesses of this foul cave, and I will decide whether they are the work of the devil!"

A look of great disappointment passed over the face of Merlin, but he turned and beckoned the knights to follow him into the cave.

"I will show you" he said "You will be struck with wonder at what I have achieved".

The knight took a torch, a long piece of wood with twine wrapped round half of it soaked in cow fat, from his horse. He struck a flint to light it, and held it up. He knew he would need it in the cave.

They moved into the shadowy recesses, until Merlin stopped at a table with several pots and tools on it.

"I want to show you this!" he said, with glee. He indicatecd a big pot with a lid. The knight bent over it. Merlin pulled the top off with a flourish.

"Arrghhhh" screamed the knight as a vapour with small particles of powder was rising slowly out of the bowl, accompanied by a foul smell.

"Old man! Close the lid! Close the lid! That is a stench worse than ten thousand corpses!"

Merlin dutifully put back the lid, but still beamed proudly.

"What in the name of all that's wonderful is in that pot?" screamed the knight, his eyes smarting.

"Mouldy bread!" exclaimed Merlin, and beamed, as if mouldy bread was as precious suddenly as gold. "Loaves and loaves of mouldy bread congealed into a mass. You ask why?" He held up his forefinger. "Because I have discovered quite by accident when some mouldy bread came in contact with filthy bandages I had taken off a wound, that the pus that issues from the wound, when put in a spoon, thrives, but when mixed with the mould from bread, it withers. Why? There is a kind of spirit in the mould of bread which will destroy all disease." His voice grew louder with excitement as he spoke. "Which will heal the wounds of all our foot soldiers on the battlefield - stop the foul fevers that plague us in the cold of winter! In the mould of old bread, is our salvation from illness!

"Why! As you may have heard, I have already tried my medicine on calves that were thought to be dead with that ague. By applying my concoction to their mouths they have, in a few days, lifted themselves to their feet, to the wonder of all, and become well"

His eyes widened as he hoped for a sign of recognition of this wonder from the knight.

But the knight only stared at Merlin with a look that could kill.

"With the foul-smelling mould on bread you will cure all our ills? You will run round the battle field with a sack of mouldy bread pasting on the wounds of our soldiers?" he sneered derisively." It would make their wounds smart and sting even more!"

Merlin only kept smiling proudly, missing the knight's sarcasm.

The knight stared at the pot, as if he was about to tip it over in disgust, then he looked at Merlin, with narrowed eyes, as if he had another plan. "Lead us on down the cave, old man, and show what else of the devil's work you have contrived."

Merlin made a face of hurt at the phrase "the devil's work" but was only too pleased to show the knight more of his projects.

The two subordinate knights only looked at each other and shrugged, as if they found Merlin's inventions incomprehensible, but diverting.

The further they moved into the cave the darker it became, so the knight was glad of his flare. They came upon another earthen pot that had a foul smelling liquid in it. It smelt like rotting lemons. As the knight approached it his eyes started to smart. In the pot were standing a sword of steel and a sword of bronze each with a chain attached to their ends. Merlin lifted up each end of the two pieces of chain in his hands. Out of the pot rose steadily, besides the smell of lemons, the pungent odour of corroding metal.

"In this pot I have the juice of more than 100 lemons" he explained. "As you have no doubt observed, when you cut a lemon with a knife, the juice eats away the iron, and it eats away bronze, too, but not so quickly. I was endeavouring to combine iron and bronze together, to get the strength of one with the resistance to rust of the other, but I have observed when I join the two swords together by a chain of iron, the iron suddenly is eaten away more and the bronze less. And furthermore, when they are joined by a chain… Watch"

The knight peered into the bowl, grimacing against the stench. There were tiny bubbles on the blade of the steel sword and on the blade of the bronze sword. Merlin held the two pieces of chain together, and sure enough, the bubbles on the steel sword increased noticeably while the bubbles on the bronze sword decreased.

"And" said Merlin, holding up his forefinger again to make the point "I detect after a time a slight warmth in the chain when this happens. The power that causes the iron to be eaten away faster, and the bronze slower, has a power to warm the chain."

The knight only glared at him.

"Why, a force is here that will heat our houses, and move men if only it could be harnessed and multiplied one million times. We need only a strong enough nectar such as comes from the lemon, and swords of the right metal ….."

"So a thousand pots of lemon juice and a thousand rusty swords will heat our houses will they, old man?" derided the knight.

The look of disappointment at the knight's sarcasm again came over Merlin's face. But he was not deterred, he led the knight even further on down the cave. A steaming pot was cooking over a fire.

"What is this, old man?" said the knight.

"You see the steam form the water in the pot as it boils? What does it do?"

"Tell me, old man, what does it do?" said the knight, becoming more and more irritated with the old man's enthusiasm over such trivial things.

"It moves the lid. It pushes the lid up so it can get out. I have tried a big stone on the lid to hold it down, but if there is enough steam being made it will lift the stone!

"There is a force here, that, if harnessed, could move men, could move boats! Could power a cutting saw so it could fell a tree as fast as ten men. A force that could pull a plough without horses! A force that could pump water from wells! That could pull a carriage without horses!"

"So we should let our horses go and carry pots of steaming water that will propel us, should we, old man?" said the knight sarcastically.

Once again Merlin made a grimace of disappointment, but then turned and led them further on down the cave.

There was another pot on a table. It was tied to the table, and a piece of string was trailing out of it. There was a lid on the pot. There was also a kind of pipe made from a hollow reed going into the pot.

"I discovered this astonishing thing when I was blowing on some meat that I was cooking in oil, to blow some dust off it, and some of the oil went into the flames of the fire and exploded" said Merlin. "This string is joined to a flint, that will strike against another flint inside the pot when I pull it and make a spark. Watch me, I am going to inject a mixture of cooking oil and air into the pot by blowing it through this reed, then I will pull the string and strike the flint".

Merlin picked up a cup that the knight could tell was full of some sort of oil pressed from seeds, he took a mouthful, making a face the same time, for it tasted foul, then he put his mouth to the reed and blew it into the pot. Simultaneously he pulled the string to strike the flint, and there was a small "bang" and the lid of the pot lifted up to relieve the pressure of the exploding oil and air mixture.

"The explosion causes the lid to jump up!" said Merlin, his eyes glowing, "Just as does boiling steam. The tighter fits the lid, with more force it jumps up. If this could be caused to happen over and over again constantly, the force of the explosion could be harnessed to move chariots, ships – why, to move anything, It is only a matter of making the amount of oil and air that is blown in big enough, and the pot big enough, and number of explosions you can make to occur as quickly in succession as possible."

"So with a thousand pots of oil and a thousand men blowing through reeds on my chariot I can leave my horses at home, is that right, old man?" said the knight with great sarcasm.

"And here we have what you will recognize" Merlin went on, ignoring him in his enthusiasm.

He had a model of a windmill on the same table. He bent down and blew against the sails, and they turned.

"You know the wind makes the sails turn" he said." Has it never occurred to anyone, that if the sails are made to turn in the other direction, they would push the wind?"

"Push the wind" repeated the knight derisively, but reflecting at the same time that this was really the devil's work. "You can push the wind can you, old man?"

"Yes, I can push the wind" he said." Or to be more precise, I can create a wind! And also the sails will push water, for water is just like the wind, except it is thicker. Think of an oarsman rowing a boat, he has to push, then take the oars oat and move them back, then push again, and bring them back. Half his time is wasted, and half his strength is wasted, But the sails of the windmill, if moved opposite to the way the wind blows them will push the air constantly, and if these sails were on a boat, in the water, they would push the boat, if only there was a force to power them"

"And pray with what force would you power them?" asked the knight.

"Why!" Merlin indicated his exploding pot he had blown the oil into. "With the power of this, or" he pointed to the steam device "with the power of the steam!"

"And how pray tell would you harness the power of the steam or the power of your exploding oil-pot to the windmill which you have upside down in the water, tied to the boat?" said the knight with great sarcasm."The burning oil just produces one 'puff!' then it is gone!"

Merlin looked pained. "I have not yet devised a scheme" he said. "But!" He held up his forefinger to emphasise the "but" in a way that was beginning to ir-ritate the knight exceedingly. "I surmise if many men devoted many hours to the study of it, it could be done! Just think of this, for instance! It is an idea I have! You know the handle you turn to bring a bucket up from a well. The force of your arm turns the crank and pulls the weight of the bucket up constantly. If that "puff" from the exploding of the oil could be harnessed to push a crank just as your arms push the crank, it could turn the sails of a windmill, which if held upside down in the water, could push the boat".

"But the "puff" just happens and then goes away" opined the knight. "It would push the crank, then stop. Your idea is false".

"If" said Merlin, holding up his finger again as if he was about to make a significant point." the 'puff' could be made to happen in quick succession, over and over again, it could push the crank around continuously, and therefore propel the boat. If the 'puff' of the exploding oil could, besides pushing the crank, initiate the next "puff", that would, in turn, push the crank, and so on. This is my plan...."

Now he looked guilty at his own tardiness in solving the problem.

"....but I have not had time yet to perfect it!'

He looked down at the earthen floor of the cave, dejectedly.

Then he lifted his head again. "But if three or more explosions of the oil can be harnessed to push the crank around in one cycle, it would have constant force pushing it in its revolution. Just think of two men cutting a tree with a cross saw, one pushes, then the other pushes, then one pushes, then the other pushes, so there is no lost movement".

The knight only eyed him with contempt and impatience. Merlin raised his finger again, And had a mischievous twinkle in his eye.

"You know, some of my most wonderful discoveries, have been by accident – I cannot always claim intuition".

He reached over to a table, a lifted off a lump of a soft, damp, pliable substance that he could knead in his hand like clay.

"Feel it!' he offered the knight, holding it towards him.

The knight scowled at Merlin, and slowly put out his hand and put two of his fingers lightly on the strange, soft lump then drew them away, as if was afraid the lump might contaminate him.

"This concoction, which I discovered by accident, when mixed with water, will clean dirt of the skin 100 times better than mere water. When mixed with water it creates a foam, which when applied to the body, separates the dirt from the skin and when washed off with pure water, leaves the skin unbelievably pure and soft. You know how in summer we sweat, and dirt sticks to out sweat, well this substance dissolves the sweat from the skin and thereby takes away the dirt. I happened to be boiling oil in a pot, and scooping potash out of the fire accidentally spilled it in the oil, and thought nothing of it, until I observed later this substance floating on the top, It has no characteristics of oil or of potash, but it is engendered by boiling them together, A miracle! A cleaning agent like we have never known,. You know our queen is renowned for the whiteness and softness of her skin? Well, if she were to bathe in water mixed with this miraculous substance, it would be even softer."

"You propose to have our Queen bathe in a vat of potash and oil, do you, old man?' said the knight, staring him down with a sly accusing grin, with an air of having found yet another revelation of Merlin's perfidy. "Are you intent on denigrating our royal house with your wizardry!"

Merlin was shocked.

"No! No! No! The substance is made from oil and potash, but it is neither oil nor potash. It is created by a miraculous conjunction of them both, but has the characteristics of neither,.."

Then, when he saw the knight was still beyond convincing, his demeanour changed and he started on a new tack.

"Good knight" he said, with a gleam in his eye. "Would you say I could conjure up a ghost?"

The knight's expression now changed from suspicion to one of fear, and his hand closed over the handle of his sword in his scabbard, as if, if a spirit appeared, he wanted to be ready

Merlin just grinned at him as if he was still hiding a joke.

"Would you say I could capture my own voice, and then have it speak back to you again?"

The knight now frowned. He kept his hand on his sword, as if he was afraid Merlin was about to conjour up a demonic force greater than his own force of steel.

"I have observed" said Merlin "that the branches of the tree whistle when the wind blows through them because the movement of the air makes them vibrate, and vibration is sound. I have observed, that the reed within a hunting horn vibrates, and that makes a note.

"I have observed, that when we speak" he touched his finger to the front of his neck "something within our own neck vibrates.

"I have observed that when a thrush sings his neck vibrates, So I surmise that vibration is sound, and sound is vibration. I have further observed that a powerful singer can shatter a glass of crystal if it is held before his mouth when he reaches a certain note. I surmise therefore, that sound can cause vibration of objects. If that vibration could be made into a signature, and then that signature could cause a vibration, why it would produce the same sound again!

"I discovered this when I was sitting under a thorn tree. The whistling wind blew the branch of the tree and scratched my arm. Before I could draw away it blew again and caused an even bigger cut in my arm. So the whistling wind left its mark as a cut because of the fortuitous presence of the thorn. Therefore the whistling wind left its signature, as it were, of its sound on my arm.

"Watch"

Merlin drew the knight's attention to a tube, fashioned in the shape of a hunting horn, that he had made of parchment. In the narrow end of the parchment was stuck through a long thorn. The end with the thorn rested on a cylindrical piece of wood that had been honed to an almost perfect circular shape. It was held in its centre at each end and one end had a handle so it could be turned. The wood was covered with what looked like candle wax. There were paths cut in the wax at one end. Merlin picked up the tube and place it on the waxed piece of wood where there were not tracks He put his head to the mouth of the tube, and shouted in as loud a voice as he could "All praise our king!" turning the handle slowly as he did, and pushing the thorn gently to the side at the same time, so the thorn cut a circular track along the waxed piece of wood. Then he picked up the end of the tube with the thorn in it and moved it back to where he had started. He then said to the knight

"Put you ear against Imst the end of the tube into which I talked and listen closely. Hold your breath while you do it so there will be maximum silence!"

The knight gave Merlin a sour look as if it was a great infringement of his dignity to submit to such tomfoolery, but he did so. Merlin turned the handle, and faintly but surely the knight heard the echo of Merlin's voice chanting "All praise our king". The knight's eyes widened. This was surely witchcraft!

"The voice of our king could be preserved for ever, so he could speak to his subjects long after he is gone! Our pipers and lute players and choirs could preserve their music so that when they are no long with us we could hear it. The voice of our king could be carried by this means to our soldiers in battle, and let them hear it and thereby gain encouragement to continue the fight…"

The knight was convinced now the old man was conjuring up ghosts. What else could speak out of a piece of wood, a tube of parchment, and a thorn?

"So, with this contrivance, you could hear the spirits of the dead, could you, old man?" he asked pointedly, as if he has already made up his mind that that was so, but wanted to hear it from Merlin's mouth.

Merlin made a face of uncomprehension, as if he did not understand why the knight did not understand.

"Well…I suppose..in a way…you could hear the voice of the long-dead……yes…but…they are not the voices of the dead…only the voices of the living, preserved……long after they are dead."

The knight bent down and put his face close to Merlin's. "Old man, I have seen enough!"

The knight then straightened up and his eyes then wandered up and down the cave, at all the contraptions he had seen. He was not listening to Merlin who was now trying to explain the mechanism by which the voice preserving machine worked. He looked back at Merlin and was about to say something, when Merlin moved away and came back with a fistful of pages of parchment.

"All this I have written down, with detailed drawings, and detailed instructions as to how my devices can be built" he explained. "Why, there is knowledge here that could give us victory over all our foes, that could make us masters of all the land! That would make us master over the seasons, the cold, the heat of the summer, the floods, the droughts, the pestilences...."

The knight looked at the other two knights meaningfully, and then at the parchments with sly interest. "Old man" said the knight."Have you made any copies of this parchment?"

Merlin looked at him curiously, wondering why he should ask.

"Old man, has anyone else built such devilment as you have?"

"Why, no" answered Merlin, curious as to why he should ask.

The knight snatched the parchments from Merlin's hand and to the dismay of Merlin he held the parchment to the torch flame until it caught alight. Merlin tried to snatch it way, but the other two knights grabbed him and held him back, He was a physically feeble old man so it was easy to restrain him. The knight grinned at Merlin while he held the burning parchment in his hands until the flames neared his fingers, whereupon he dropped it onto the earthen floor where it continued burning.

"Old man, do you see how easily the work of the devil can be turned into smoke" he boasted, looking down at the charred remains.

Merlin's face writhed in horror.

"All my work! All my knowledge gone up in smoke1 You have destroyed what could have helped all men everywhere. You are a fool!"

The knight stuck him across the head with the handle of his sword and Merlin screamed in pain and sunk onto his knees..

"I'm a fool old man, am I? No, old man, You are an agent of the devil! Doing the devil's work! You are a fool, for thinking you could get away with it."

He kicked the table with the model windmill on it with all his might and it all fell to the floor. He stamped on the windmill with his big boot and smashed it. He walked back to the oil-pot and pushed over the table it was on. He kicked over the table with the pot that was steaming. He kicked over the pot with the lemon juice and swords and the pot of bread mould.

When the destruction was complete he stood with his sword by his side and glared at Merlin. Merlin was still crouched on the ground, holding his head where the knight had struck him, like a stricken bird.

"Do you know what you have done? All these wonderful machines I have built that could have benefited mankind! Now I will have to build them again"

The knight frowned at him.

"But I have burnt your parchments, old man. You cannot build them without your parchments".

"It is all in my head" said Merlin. "I can rebuild. But all the details I will have to work out again. I wrote the parchment so that others could use my knowledge!".

"So I have not destroyed the devil's work by destroying these contraptions" the knight thought out loud. "In that case there is only one thing for it."

He turned to the two other knights.

"Hold him!"

The two other knights grabbed Merlin,. While he drew his enormous sword from its sheath and plunged it into Merlin's chest. The two knights, despite the slaughter and blood they had seen on the battlefield, made expressions of horror at their leader's deadly act, though they still held hold of Merlin. For a second Merlin's face assumed a look of horror, then his eyes closed and he fell back while blood gushed from him. The two knights dropped the corpse to the ground.

The knight looked at the stricken Merlin until he was sure he was quite dead, then led the two others to the mouth of the cave.

"I have slain the devil!" he said gleefully to the other two knights as they walked among the debris of broken pots and devices. "He lies in there with the remains of all his evil work! The king will be proud of me!"

"But another could rebuild all the devilment from the ruins, perhaps" surmised on of the knights. Is there no way we could seal this devilment up for ever?"

The knight frowned thoughtfully as they reached the mouth of the cave. "You are right" he said. His eyes went up to the rocky formations that covered the side of the mountain above. "We must seal the cave."

He started climbing up the rocks. "Follow me!" he cried.

The three knights climbed up to the top of the peak. The were great boulders and loose rocks everywhere.

"Move these great boulders - they will start a land-slide that will cover the cave for all time" he said.

He got behind one and started pushing. "Help me" he said.

The three of them proceeded to push boulders down the side of the hill, which soon became a landslide. One boulder pushed another and the avalanche of rocks multiplied as it got lower. The mouth of the cave was soon covered., and then buried behind a small mountain of rocks. When there were no more to be moved, the knight led the other two down to the ground again.

They stood in front of the mountain of rocks that now blocked the cave. The knight said "The weather will bring more rocks and earth down as the years go by, and seal the cave even more securely. The devilment will be hidden for ever. Not for hundreds of years will this cave ever be opened. Mouldy bread curing disease! Steam pushing boats! Exploding oil driving machines! Our Queen washing with a concoction of oil boiled with potash…Windmills upside down in the sea pushing boats! Voices trapped in wax… Hearing the voices of the dead long after they have departed this world..Today is the year of our Lord 541. For hundreds of years we will be safe from this devilment!"

He looked into the distance, and then surveyed the countryside as if wishing there were throngs of people there who would cheer him for his brave deed. Then he declared as if to those non-existent throngs "Our kingdom has no need of wizards!"

HOUSE OF ANIMALS

"Six hundred thousand dollars, and a house worth seven hundred thousand, are to be left to a dog, a cat and a snake! I don't believe it!".

The speaker was an angular-faced, impeccably groomed, intense and stern-looking young lawyer, and he was standing over his interlocutor in an attitude that demanded a rejoinder to his crisp words. He had a tone of voice that suggested he was used to getting straight answers out of people, when he fired at them direct questions.

The party he was demanding the explanation from was older, and rather more sloppily dressed, like someone who is retired and does not have to worry about his appearance. He sat slouched in his seat with an attitude of resignation, as if the ways of the world were awkward, unjust and beyond reason, but he had learned there was little could be done to usurp them. He shrugged without enthusiasm. "I told you" he whined in a tired voice. "It's not to be left to them, it's to be left to their welfare. It will provide upkeep on the house, and pay for someone to go in twice a week to feed them and take them to the vet if they get sick. My brother hates his family, and he is doing this just to spite them. There's nothing I can do about it. Is there any law says you can't leave money for the welfare of animals?"

The lawyer started pacing the room, with an air of pronouncing his valuable counsel as if it came from long years of learning and experience of which he was proud "One can bequeath one's estate to whatever and whoever one likes, provided it is not any illegal purpose, or it is not practicable. I once handled the case of an old woman who owned race-horses, and all her money was left for their welfare. But then she had no living relatives. I am of the opinion that in this case we have only one of two options, to talk the old man out of it, or get him to just leave part of his estate to the animals, or to have him declared of unsound mind. From what you say of his ideas, I am firmly of the opinion that the latter might be entirely possible. Let me interview your brother, and I might be able to either talk him out of this ridiculous bequest, or pick up some obvious mental aberration we can use to our advantage".

It was two days later that the lawyer's shiny black Mercedes pulled up outside a residence that might have once looked imposing, in harmony with the other houses in the sedate street, but now looked seedy and neglected, from what you could see of it behind the undergrowth that had overtaken the front garden. He pushed the gate open with his foot, as it only hung precariously by one rusty hinge, and fought his way along the path which had been invaded by the branches of trees and shrubs. The front verandah was littered with old newspapers, bottles and cartons, and its floorboards were rotting with gaping holes in some places. It did not look like the place of abode of a gentleman with either much money to leave anyone, or inpossession of great intellectual faculties.

He looked for a knocker or a bell, found none, and so banged firmly on the door.

After some seconds he heard a faint, croaky, sickly voice that had no strength behind it call out from inside "Open the door". He tried the handle and pushed, thinking it was himself that was being addressed, as the old man lived alone, but found it was locked. Then he suddenly felt it give way beneath his pressure as if someone inside had turned the key. However, when the door swung open an empty hall was revealed. He stepped into the dim hallway, that was wide, high, musty-smellling and crammed with all kinds of oriental furniture, stuffed animals in glass cases, mounted heads of game, native artefacts, huge, imposing old, dark portraits and landscapes in thick gilt frames and other paraphenalia. Then he started abruptly as he noticed a retriever dog at his feet, who, now he had stepped into the house, proceeded to raise itself on its hind legs and push the door shut with its paws, moving with little steps. He stared at this apparition in genuine amazement. It was not often a sight made him lose his composure, but this spectacle did. Then the croaky voice came again, louder this time now that he was inside the house, saying "Keep on down the hall, lawyer-man, and take the second doorway on the right".

He stepped down the passage through the gloom, glancing round in mystification at a collection of miscellania. It was like being in a museum, or more accurately, in the storeroom belonging to a museum, because the items were not particularly arranged with any degree of order. The dog walked right at his heels, and curiously, seemed to keep looking up at him, as if it was studying his face. He pushed open the second door along as instructed, and found himself in a room so filled with tobacco smoke you could have picked it up in shovel-fulls. This room was more brightly lit, the light coming from a single bare electric bulb, but the walls, and indeed the floor and ceiling were cluttered with an even greater profusion of stuffed animals, books, oriental weaponry and prints. In the midst of it all, in an old brass bed against one wall, propped up on pillows, was a dyspeptic, ill-humoured and cadaverous looking old man. He had long, stringy, matted grey hair, and the pale, lifeless skin of one who has not seen sunlight for months. However, he looked alert, and observant, as if he was used to having plenty of things to exercise his faculties on. He eyed the lawyer with a look of resentment, impatience, suspicion and irritation at being interrupted from his work. He had three large volumes open on his bed, and was making notes from them onto a writing pad.

"Mr Wilkinson, I presume. Let me welcome you to the "House of Animals". Find yourself a seat, if there is one. If there isn't - stand up, or sit on the floor, or whatever you like, I don't care!"

The lawyer was still gaping at it all in astonishment, and was temporarily los for words, which was unusual for him. Eventually he started with a leading statement "It appears you have an extremely well-trained dog...".

He was able to hide his feelings and turn on the sharp, precise, aggressive tone that seemed to challenge people to respond. He was so used to asserting himself he could turn it on and off like a tap. He had

had a lot of victories recently to bolster himself up. In the past fortnight he had successfully defended a drug dealer, who he had got off on the grounds that growing the plants had been a scientific experiment, and got a drunken driver who had killed someone off on only a $100 fine and three months suspension. He had the philosophy that guilt or innocence were no business of his, his job was to do the maximum for the client who was paying him.

Of course, the old man could did not know all this, and could not resist a smirk of pride at the complement directed at his ability to train animals. He put down his book and clasped his hands across his stomach, working his body more comfortably back against the pillows. "Circus tricks! That's the least of his talents". He looked the lawyer straight in the eye without flinching. "I suppose you've come to talk me out of leaving them my money."

The lawyer ascertained the old man was given to getting straight to the point and not wasting words. He liked that. He launched into the delivery he had prepared.

"I am, sir. Your plan is ridiculous, unheard of, misguided, possibly illegal, and probably impracticable. There is no guarantee, in fact, hardly any probability, that any person will be able to be found to take on the care of your animals, even for a mere few days a week, and in any case, if such a soul could be found, they could hardly have experience in attending to the needs of a dangerous snake, as I hear you have…!"

The old man held up his hand with a limp but emphatic gesture to stop him. "I've got people at the university who have already agreed to it, in exchange for my bequesting to them my library, which, I don't hesitate to boast, is one of the most exhaustive in the world on certain subjects".

The lawyer stopped in his tracks, for he had been pacing up and down, and a look of displeasure passed over his face, at being stumped on that one. But he then went on: "And I might also say I doubt the actual legality of harbouring poisonous snakes, in anything but a zoological establishment. And in addition insurance cannot be got on any house unoccupied for a period of time, and occupation by animals is not, I might tell you, classified as 'being occupied'....."

Once he got wound up he was in great spirit, shooting out his words with powerful delivery, like the bullets from a machine gun, but as he spoke on, he saw the old man raise his head forward slightly from the pillow, open his eyes wide, and nod slowly in a sarcastic mockery of dutiful attention. Then suddenly the old man interrupted the flow of words.

"My brother put you up to this, didn't he?". The young lawyer stopped again abruptly, nonplussed.

"I have had an interview with your brother recently, yes…"

"They're - not - getting - anything". He spaced the words out with as much terseness and emphasis as his shaky old voice could summon.

"Mr Wilkinson. I have a daughter who hasn't spoken to me for eighteen years. Eighteen years, can you imagine that? She thinks her father is a disgusting, eccentric, mad old man. My wife was a witch. As for my brother, well, he just takes their side anyway, so he's not getting anything either.

"When I did my thesis for my doctorate in zoology, I did it on a subject that had fascinated me: communication among animals. The more I learned about this subject, the more fascinated I became, and the more I wanted to learn. And what was the next logical step to the study of communication among animals? Why, communication between different species, and between humans and animals. You made me smile just now when you complimented that mutt on his circus trick of standing up on his hind legs and closing the door. Do you know why I smiled? Because one thing that struck me as fantastic when I first began this study, was the realisation was how little attention science has paid to this question, and how the "research" on this subject, since the dawn of civilization, has been only of the empirical kind, as much as people have need for everyday use: how you teach a sheep dog to herd sheep, making a parrot talk, teaching police dogs to chase burglars, pekinese strutting round with bows in their hair in circus rings, and so on. Ugh! Kids' stuff. So I had the honour of virtually being not only a world authority, but a pioneer in a science I myself created. I spent my entire working life in academic work. I was a professor at 35. Then, after I retired, I devoted twenty five years to training animals, to seeing just how much knowledge I could stuff into their skulls, how many skills I could impart to them. You were surprised that a dog could open a door. That mutt can open any door in the house. Don't you notice how all the door knobs have been replaced with lever shaped handles? Mr Wilkinson, that dog cannot only open doors, it can understand over two thousand different English words, and comprehend sentences made out of any combination of them. It can also read". The lawyer shuddered perceptibly. "It can look at a clock and tell the time, and perform some task I have instructed it to at a given hour. It can understand the mi-aouings of the cat, and the hissings of the snake, and can give instructions in turn to them, via its own barkings and snarlings. It can carry out complicated tasks, like turning the dial on the radio until it finds the right station. Watch this." He turned to the dog.

The lawyer's attention drawn to the animal, which was seated on its haunches in the corner of the room, and he now noticed for the first time, something peculiar about it. It was watching him. It wasn't looking at him, it was watching him. When his eyes met the dog's, its eyes in turn suddenly narrowed defensively, as if had been caught out. Go to the bookcase and get me the dictionary". The old man spoke to the dog with emphatic, measured tones, but otherwise as you would talk to a person. The dog stood up and walked to the bookcase, and stood on its hind legs, surveying the titles. An eerie feeling came over the young lawyer. The dog did not move with alacrity like a performing dog, but with a strange human quality, slowly, begrudgingly, dutifully, and with a curious aura of being bored with the whole process. It bent its head sideways and dragged a book out with its teeth. The the old man instructed "Not that one. The big one on the shelf below". The dog dutifully pushed it back with its nose, and took another volume from the lower shelf. It brought it over to its master and stood by the bed holding the book between its teeth, as if waiting to be told what to do next. "Drop it on the chair over there" instructed the old man, and the dog dutifully did what it was told.

"It's a curse having an educated dog sometimes" the old man opined with exaggerated coolness. "Whenever it gets a different brand of pet food it reads the label to see what's in it first, and if it doesn't like what it sees, it refuses to eat the food". He looked at the lawyer as if challenging him not to believe his words.

"The more interested I became in my work, which became my life's obsession, the more I came to lose interest in humans. I hate people! I haven't met one person yet who hasn't at some stage let me down. No doubt this is partly a failing on my part for being demanding and irascible. Nevertheless, there it is, I hate people." There was genuine, spiteful bitterness in his tone as he spoke. "I've never met a soul yet who really appreciates my work. Most people want to make a circus act out of it. I've got a few associates overseas I correspond with... but if I met them I'd probably hate them too....I hope people really smart when they hear all my money's going to the animals.

"Not that the animals like me any better. They despise me, do you know that? Why wouldn't they? What servant likes his master? They're only waiting for me to die. But they know which side their bread's buttered on. They know they're due to get the lot. For that they don't mind being loyal underlings, for so long as it takes."

The old man appeared to have said his fill for a time, and the lawyer had been too deflated to counter attack yet, so there was a pause.

"You want coffee?"

"Well, I can see you are incapacitated......"

"Oh, it's all right. The dog will make it".

He looked towards the dog. "Get two coffees".

Wilkinson's draw dropped again as the dog trotted off. He heard in a distant room the sound of a bubbling urn start up. Then the dog came back and barked once.

"He says do you take sugar?". The old man was beaming with malicious pride.

"Ah, yes, ah - two". Wilkinson was trying to sound nonchalant.

A minute later the dog came back again, and barked twice.

"Milk? he wants to know".

"Ah, no...."

"I suggest you go and bring it in yourself. He can carry cups, but he usually spills some of it".

Wilkinson followed the dog to the kitchen, feeling for the first time in years like a twerp, like someone who was being made a spectacle of, though there was no one there to see his predicament. In the kitchen he found that the dog on its hind legs again, pushing a mug, with its nose, under the tap on an urn, and pushing the tap, on the urn to turn it on. He took the mug away when it was full, and the dog slunk away with a look of resentful servility. Yes, there was no question, that dog had a personality. It gave you looks, and it surveyed you, as if it was trying to see what made you tick.

Back in the old man's bedroom, he stood and sipped his coffee, while the old man ruminated with a resentful look on his face.

"You been doing law-work...all the time?" he asked, with a vague air of just trying to make conversation as if the uneasy silence was annoying him.

The lawyer seemed to revitalise with the subject being changed to his own metier. "Fifteen years. I am a senior partner in one of the most dynamic firms in Sydney". The old man shrugged and lifted one side of his lip, as if to say, "is that supposed to impress me?"

"Good business to be in?" he then enquired with the same bored air.

"Excellent! I believe there is nothing like the competition, the battles, the do-or-die, the pressure, the knife-edge or the importance of attention to detail in legal practice for bringing out what's best in a man". He was now emphasising his words by making gestures with a clenched fist. "And we are professional: professional in thought, professional in deed, professional in action, professional in outlook, to the finest detail, and because we are professional, we are highly successful". He spat out the words 'professional' and 'successful' with an aggressive emphasis on the second syllables, as if the words were barbs, supposed to wound. "We know our business, we find and exploit know the weaknesses in our opponents, and when we know them, we move in for the kill, and they are led like lambs to the slaughter. We demand the utmost of our staff, and we don't tolerate dunderheads!". He was quite carried away, at being given this opportunity to blow his own trumpet.

The spiel was annoying the old man. He squirmed and looked this way and that in unease, almost wishing he could put the snake onto him, and wondered if there was anything in his legal books that could counter that. However he did the next best thing, he rolled his body slightly and, just as the young man got to the climax of a sentence, loudly farted, as if to say, 'and that's what I think of lawyers'.

The lawyer stopped abruptly, half disgusted, half nonplussed. The old man turned his face away slightly, and covered his mouth with the edge of the sheet to hide his giggles, like a schoolboy who has been caught out.

"Sorry" he said eventually. "I'm and old man…. I got trouble… weakness…I can't help it….."

When his giggles had subsided he looked at the dog, and said "Tell The Cat to come".

The dog put its nose round the bedroom door and barked once.

"And tell her to bring me a new packet of smokes". To communicate this instruction the dog barked an extrafive times. Sure enough a few moments later a cat appeared, its jaws stretched around a packet of cigarettes. It jumped on the bed and dropped them under her master's nose, then jumped back to the floor, arched her back in boredom, stretched her front legs, and ambled lazily to the door.

"Stay awhile" the old man halted her, and the cat stopped. "I've got to show this gentleman how÷ smart you are." The cat turned round and closed and opened its eyes slowly as if acknowledging the command but saying "how tedious".

"What's fourteen minus eight" he asked her.

The cat dutifully miaowed six times.

"What's twenty per cent of forty?"

The cat miaowed eight times.

He thrust one of the books he had been working from under the cat's nose. "Find page 341 in this book".

The cat turned the pages of the book awkwardly with a paw and its nose, until she found the appropriate page.

"Go to the piano and play the scale of B flat".

The lawyer noticed for the first time there was indeed an upright piano in the shadows at one end of the room, and he watched the cat jump up on top of it, and stretching its paw over the edge, hit the correct notes, with great effort admittedly, of the right scale.

The lawyer found it hard to meet the old man's gaze. He no longer knew what to think. He had heard and seen so much that he did not understand.

Suddenly the old man looked towards the door, drew back his lips, and made a peculiar hissing sound. Within a few seconds the lawyer saw something come round the doorway and slither across the carpet that made him cringe back. It was a snake, beautifully black, shiny and about five feet long. The lawyer took two quick steps backward from its path. "There's no need to jump away" the old man commented calmly.

"But it's a snake!" He said it as if the old man hadn't noticed.

"I know. A very deadly snake. One bite from that and you'd be no more. I use it as a watch-snake".

"What do mean, a watch snake?"

"It guards the house, just like a watch dog, but much more effective. It can get through tiny spaces, move quicker than any man or beast, hide anywhere, glide up on you silently, and when it kills, it kills without any mess. But don't worry, there's no danger it will molest you. It only attacks when I tell it, or in defence of any part of this property."

"What do you do? Point at it and shout 'Kill!'?"

"Shhhhhh! You might set it off. It's something very like that, believe it or not... But watch this."

He drew his lips back again and hissed at the snake. "I'm telling it to make a circle round you three times, he explained. Sure enough, to the lawyer's horror, it slithered quickly three times round the lawyer's feet and returned to where it had been.

"Crawl through his legs and make a circle round one of his feet".

After giving this instruction he hissed again. The snake dutifully did as it was instructed - while Wilkinson shivered, it slithered between his legs and made a perfect circle round one of his feet joining its mouth to its tail.

"Now curl up on top of the bookcase" he instructed, and then hissed. It was obvious the English translation was only for the lawyer's benefit, and the snake had to be communicated with in its own tongue. The snake shot away, shot up the bookcase and curled into a little, innocent package on top of it.

"I'd like to make a phone call". The lawyer said this as if he wanted any excuse to get out of that room. The old man made a generous motion with his hand in the direction of the door as if to say "Be my guest", and said to the dog "Show our... guest thephone, please".

The lawyer found himself following the dog out the door, and into another room. A phone was on the table there. He put his attache case on the table and rifled through it for some papers, but then saw the dog was sitting in the corner watching him. He felt ridiculous, but he glared at it trying to imply it should leave, which it eventually did, though of course this couldn't stop it eavesdropping from outside.

He looked up a phone number and talked on the phone in whispered tones so the old man could surely not hear.

The gist of what he said to whoever he had on the other end of the line, was that although he had not got anywhere with talking the old man out of his plan, he was sure he could see several ways of outwitting the old man's wishes. He was sure if they could only get him away from the house for the purposes of an examination by a psychologist, (perhaps he could be persuaded to do this under the guise of being examined to confirm his sanity rather than disprove it), whatever doctor examined him, once he started talking about his trained animals, would be convinced, not being able to see for himself, that he was not of sound mind. Also, there was the possibility of actually taking the animals out of the old man's hands while he was alive on the ground of cruelty to animals. And he enunciated several other ways in which he was sure he could fulfil his client's brief.

But when he put the receiver down, and turned to put his phone book back in his attache case, there was the cat standing up in it rifling through his papers, and peering closely at them like a short sighted person trying to read fine print. He pushed it away with a curse and it squealed and jumped off the table.

Then he caught the briefest glimpse of the dog's head visible in the slight space between the door, which was slightly ajar, and the jamb. The dog ran away as soon as he moved a step, but could it be? He had been talking softly, but then, dogs had a very acute sense of hearing. But the old man had had to talk slowly and deliberately to give the dog simplest instructions. No, it couldn't be!

He went back into the bedroom, where the old man had already resumed his work. He adopted a breezy air he could switch on at a moment's notice, because he had no longer any need to try to bend the old man's will in any way whatsoever.

"Well sir, I have seen enough to ascertain you are committed to your plan¡ I believe it's highly unorthodox, misguided, butcommendable for your determination. Having failed, yes I admit to having failed, I bid you good-day, thank you for your... entertainment, and...."

Meanwhile the dog ran into the room where the cat was, made one bark, motioned with his head towards the door, and then darted out again. The cat sprang up and followed. The snake was curled up in a corner of the hall, and when the dog gave it the same bark, it uncurled and shot across the floor following its two companions. They all entered a room at the back of the house. The dog pushed the door shut with its nose, then sat before the other two. It barked and growled viciously for about five minutes. At certain stages the cat would spring up, scurry frantically round the room and squeal like it was in heat at the dog's words, as if beside itself. The snake hissed incessantly, and shot to and fro across the floor, as if overflowing with anger and by its wild movements trying to expend its excess energy. Finally there was a minute of silence, and the three creatures stood still as if deciding something, then the snake reared itself up like a cobra and made a prolonged speech of vehement hisses. This was followed by a session of barking from the dog, and miaows from the cat, while both the four footed creatures looked intently at the reptile. Then they returned to the old man's bedroom.

They had decided.

The lawyer had a self satisfied smile as his picked his attache case up off the table. He had the vague sensation it was heavier than he remembered, but put that down to tiredness as the last stressful thirty minutes, and reflected that stress often took its toll in physical ways. He walked from the house, threw it into the back seat of his car and drove off.

Half an hour later he entered the front door of his home. It was an excellent apartment, everything in it was modern, fresh, of the best quality, convenient. In the centre of the room was a modular lounge upholstered in resplendent black leather; before it stood and enormous coffee table, as large as most peoples' dining tables, in black marble; there were large, tasteful, avand-garde prints set in gold and silver coloured frames on the walls that created an aura of space, airiness, and perfumed meadows, fifteen storeys above the city streets; there were trendy, "open planning" modular shelving units with every kinds of stereo equipment, video recorders and a bizarrely shaped phone that could do everything except talk back to you. Nothing could have been a greater contrast to the eccentric, old-world, cluttered residence he had just left. He went to the kitchen and got himself a beer. The kitchen was done in woodgrain and white tiles. It had everything that opened, shut or turned. He came back into the lounge, opened his attache case and took out some papers, lay back on the black leather sofa, pressed a button on the phone to dial a number automatically, kicked off his shoes, loosened his tie and sipped his beer while he waited for an answer.

When a voice answered he said "I went to see the old man. I have never in my life seen anything like I have seen today. I'm still not sure I haven't been dreaming...."

While he spoke, he did not see the papers in his attache case moving as a tiny reptilean head pushed its way to where it could hear the better. He was not aware that a slithery, black creature was stirring under the papery contents of the case as it tried to relieve the pressure it had been subjected to by stowing itself into such a confined space.

"There's no way we'll make the old futzer change his mind. This leaves the more drastic, second alternative, to fight it on the grounds of not being of sound mind, and I can tell you Michael, I am convinced we'll win…"

He did not see the black form appear over the edge of the case, and slither down the leg of the table and across the floor. He did not see, until he heard a slight brushing sound from under the coffee table, and looked down. And when he looked down, he saw the snake. The next thing his conversant on the other end of the line was:

"Aaaaarggh. Michael! there's a snake in my room!"

He had jumped to his feet and was standing with precarious balance on the lounge sofa.

"A what?"

"A snake, I'm telling you. A snake!" It made a dart for him and he jumped backward over the back of the lounge onto the floor, still clutching the phone.

"How could there be a snake in your room? You're fifteen storeys up in the middle of the city?"

"I'm telling you there's a snake in my room! It's……..aaaarrrggh! I know what it is - it's that bloody snake from that old man's house! It's followed me here! It's coming towards me!" He started darting this way and that, like somrone dodging tackles on a football field.

"Well run out the door!"

"It's between me and the door"

"Well jump out the window!"

"How can I jump out the window, I'm fifteen storeys up!"

"Well throw something at it".

The man on the end of the phone heard something bang, as if his friend had taken his advice.

"It's no good. You can't kill snakes by throwing things at them! It's coming towards me! Michael! Michael! Help me! Send someone to help me! It's coming for me!"

"Lie down and keep completely still and it will just crawl over you".

"What do you mean 'lie down and keep still?' It's here to get me! Michael! Michael! Send someone to help me! It's coming for me! Aaarrggh! Get away you fucking bastard! Aarrghhh……."

From the other end of the line came a voice. "You there? You there? Hey! Charles! Hello? Hello? You there? What's happening…"

But in the lonely apartment fifteen storeys above the city streets, no living soul remained to answer him. The last act had been played out and the lawyer had lost, beaten by the animals who had taken their revenge on the one who designed to do them out of their inheritance. Beaten by the occupants of the House of Animals!

THE ATTACK OF THE GRIL PEOPLE

"I LIKE GRILS!"

On the grimy wall of the dishevelled railway station building, someone had chalked these words. Alone under the pallid station lights, shivering in the cold, at two thirty in the morning, having nothing else on which to focus his attention, he stared at the grotesque graffiti in wonder.

The lateness of the hour, the cold, the forlorn aspect of the empty platform, seemed to create a little ambiance all their own - a pot-pourri of off-beat images framing the three words into what, he could imagine, if someone had a camera, and knew all about illumination, and angles, and lights and shadows, would win a prize in a photographic competition. He could imagine a beatnik poet writing a savage, bitter sonnet on it, or penning a rambling surrealistic essay on why anyone should go to the trouble of scrawling such an inane message on a public wall, and be so careless as to mis-spell it. Even the exclamation mark was fascinating. Somehow it lent to the letters an earnestness that would have been lacking without it. "Grils". He turned the single syllable word, that was not a real word, over and over in his mind as if it had a sort of morbid fascination. It was a grotesque word, a mutation, a word deformed and hideous. He reflected that perhaps it was because the nearest word to it was "ghoul", or maybe "grille", as in the bars of a cage, or of a prison.

A distant rumble and rattle came upon his ears and drew rapidly nearer. The train was coming. Not before time. He had been stamping in the cold for twenty five minutes.

He stepped into the nearest carriage. It was empty. In addition to that, it was the dirtiest, most abominable carriage he had ever ridden in. Orange-peel, cans, plastic bags, wrappers, sheets of newspaper, crumbs and crusts littered the floor. Every seat was slashed. Two seats had had the backs completely taken out and, presumably, thrown out of the carriage. There was dampness in one corner and down one seat the source of which he preferred not to speculate on. Obscene words had been scratched in the paint on the walls, and on the seat backs. The covers over the light bulbs hung down and swayed to and fro with the motion of the train, causing alternate light and shadow to pass rhythmically side to side across the carriage with the motion of the train. That distinctive metallic smell that you only get in the carriages of electric trains, and which clings to after you have left them, hung heavy in the air. Altogether, his surroundings were disgusting, unpleasant, unsavoury and did nothing to heighten his mood or lessen his wish to reach his destination as quickly as possible.

He huddled in a corner and stared out at the lights going past, bracing himself to be unconscious of his surroundings and to count the seventeen stations one by one as he rattled towards home.

A scrap of newspaper blew up against his feet. He picked it up aiming to read it and distract his thoughts from the unpleasant surroundings. It was part of a headline. It said

"Man Mugged on Train".

He read further:

"Last night five youths assaulted and bashed a man on a west-bound train. He was stabbed six times, bashed unconscious and then flung from the carriage. He sustained severe head, back, neck, leg and hip injuries and died later in hospital…."

He flung it back on the floor. Of all the things he could have picked up to read….

There was a discarded women's magazine on the seat beside him. Maybe that would have something more cheering in it, even it were only an interview with a film-star. He opened it at a random page.

He read "In a heart-warming story of courage and devotion this week we interview the wife of a man who was left totally paralysed after being savagely beaten by a gang of thugs on a midnight train....She has said she will devote the rest of her life to looking after him......"

He threw it down in disgust.

He picked up another page of newspaper. The first thing he read was "Crime wave hits city. Assaults on the public transport system are up by 40 per cent his year...."

In anger he screwed it up and threw it on the floor as well.

He wished there were someone else in the carriage. Preferably a big, thickset labouring man going home from work, minding his own business, quietly reading a newspaper, but who would be handy in a fight.

Then, he saw something move out of the corner of his eye. He turned his head, and just for an instant, glimpsed the most grotesque and abominable face he had ever laid eyes on staring at him from round the doorway that led to the main part of the carriage. In the brief time it stayed in view, he had an impression of hideous deformity, a bulbous nose that seemed to point in three directions at once and eyes that didn't line up, one seeming to be set higher than the other. Then the grotesque face vanished.

Panic surged inside him, and he felt his pulse begin to race. With what kind of weirdo was he trapped alone in a carriage, at two-thirty in the morning? He had been sure the carriage was empty. That could only mean that the freak he had seen had been hiding! That was all the worse. For what but some nefarious purpose could anyone be hiding in a train carriage? Only one chance seemed to work in his favour. From the height of the face above the floor, it looked like whoever the weirdo was he was a midget, so perhaps he would be able to handle him if it came to a struggle.

All these thoughts were racing through his mind, when the gruesome face reappeared, and to his horror, another appeared above it, like one of those shots from "The Three Stooges" where they all put their heads round a corner together. But whereas the first face had been hideously twisted, the second face was perfectly symmetrical. The only thing was, it was pasty-white, albino in fact, and had a pair of the most monstrous, projecting ears imaginable, and a pointed head, bald except for a tuft of white hair growing from its top, mohawk style. But the grotesqueness of this face did not end there. It had no chin. That is to say, from the mouth down, what should have been a chin just receded back and seemed to merge into the neck, with hardly a perceptible change of direction that could have been called a jaw. Before he could speculate anymore on the physiognamy of the two apparitions, the second one said to the other

"Do you think he likes us?"

The first face stared at the terror-struck traveller intently. "I think maybe he does. He was standing in front of the sign. Maybe it was him that wrote it. He stood looking at it for a full five minutes. I watched him. He didn't try to rub it out".

Then, as if they realised suddenly he was looking at them, they whipped their heads back out of sight.

He was shuddering. So there were two of them. That put them definitely at an advantage. His only chance now was that the second one looked on the scrawny side, as if a push might send him sprawling. He only wished he had something he could use as a weapon - an attache case or an umbrella. An umbrella would be good, he would thrust it like a spear directly at the throat of one of them, but he had nothing. Maybe if he hit the tall one really hard, he could knock him senseless, then grab the midget, swing him like a sack of potatoes, and throw him out of the train. He was convinced these two were not ordinary muggers; they could not be got rid of just by throwing them his wallet and saying "Listen. There's $100 in there. Just leave me alone". No. He was sure they were after something different.

There was something malevolent about them. They would be after kicks, in more ways than one. They looked like psychos. Maybe they had just escaped from some low-security funny farm. Probably their mentality was as warped and misshapen as their heads. Hiding under seats at two thirty in the morning waiting for a lonely, unsuspecting passenger to walk in - what manner of being did things like that? Oh, when would the next station come?

But what happened next, just when he had mapped out his strategy for dealing with two of the blighters, drained the blood from his face. The pair of freaks re-appeared, accompanied by not one, not two, not three not four but five more, each one as grotesque and repulsive, in its own way, as the first two. There was one of stocky build and short stature, but whose face could not be made out because it was covered with hair like a shaggy dog's; another whose eyes bulged out of their sockets like golf balls, in a way he would not have thought physically possible; another was a dwarf with a normal sized trunk but miniscule legs and arms; another had a face and hands covered with bulbous, shiny, red growths, another, a tall one, was so incredibly thin he looked like a skeleton with skin stretched over the bones.

They came in slowly, one by one, to his part of the carriage, each with his eyes fixed with apprehension on him, as if he inspired in them as much fear as they did in him. They advanced towards him in a sort of hesitant shuffle, each trying to get in for closer viewing distance, but none wishing to be at the front of the group. Then they stood staring at him with wonder and consternation. Eventually, one, the first face he had observed peering round the door, spoke.

"We don't mean you no harm, mister. We just thought maybe you liked us....."

"We saw the sign on the platform, and you standing in front of it and thought maybe it was you what wrote it" added the one whose face could not be seen for hair.

He only looked from one of them to the other, half fearful and half stupefied.

"Listen" he said eventually. "Never mind that. Just tell me, who the bloody hell are you?"

The leader looked at him solemnly, apologetically.

"We are grils".

He said it as if he was afraid to speak the word.

"Are you animal or human? Man or monster? Male or female?"

They looked from one to the other with uncomprehension, as if he had asked them a question to which there was no answer.

"We are not any of those things" said the dwarf one at last.

Then they all spoke in unison, declaring simply "We are grils".

He recoiled in horror as they shuffled nearer.

"Where the bloody hell do you all come from?"

One stepped forward, and made appealing, mournful eye-contact. "Under piles of rubble, in the dark spaces hidden deep in the tunnels, among the stagnant water, the weeds, the rubbish, the decaying leaves, the dribbling from the ends of broken pipes, under the carcasses of dead rats, where the mosquitoes and the cockroaches breed, wherever it is dank, dark, rotting, smelly and in shadow, wherever slimy things unmentionable crawl, there we live".

"In sewers, cracks, dead tree trunks, old concrete, piles of gravel. We never dare show ourselves for fear we will be hated for what we look like" stated another.

"We are afraid that if we are ever seen, no-one will like us".

He looked from one misshapen repulsive, pathetic form to the other. He was no longer as fearful of them as he was before.

"Could you really blame them?"

The one who had first put his head around the doorway of the carriage looked dumbfounded.

"You mean, you don't like us?"

"Frankly, taking all things into consideration, I would say...No!"

The short one looked unbelievably mortified, and turned to the others in horror. He looked in their faces one by one, and said in a dead monotone "He doesn't like us after all".

There was silence for some moments, and the train traveller had the sensation that it was like the time between the lighting of a fuse, and the explosion of a bomb.

Then the phrase was repeated from one and another of them in whispers, like the incantations of a prayer, that has to be intoned again and again for its meaning to be drummed into the brain: "He doesn't like us... he doesn't like us.... he doesn't like us.....". Then it seemed to change into "No-one likes us. no-one likes us...no-one likes us..." From a whisper it slowly increased in volume and passion, until they were all squealing, screeching and wailing in the last extremities of misery. "No-one like us.... no one likes us... we are grils...we are grils... we are grils... we are grils.... we are condemned for ever to be reviled.....we are grills...no-one likes us....we are grils.....we are grils....we are grils......"

Then the words started to become incomprehensible and they changed from words to a continuous wailing sound. The creatures all threw their heads back and with closed eyes began swaying from side to side as they wailed. Then, after some minutes of this, the leader of the group suddenly ran to the centre of the carriage, and started banging its head against the metal bars as if he was trying to break his skull.

Then another started running up and down the carriage, beating his head against the seats, throwing himself on the floor and smashing his forehead into it, bashing his head against the bars, throwing himself round like an acrobatic clown determined to drive the blood out through the top of his head. Another fell to the floor and lay screaming as if in a fit, and tearing his own hair out at the roots; another ran back and forth ripping his clothes to shreds with his hands and teeth, and scattering the remnants each side of him; the short one he had first seen sunk his teeth into the brass handle of the door and gnawed it until he began breaking them; they all moved with such erratic speed, they seemed to run this way and that with such sudden changes of direction, that it was as if there were 107 of them, instead of seven. It was like being locked in a padded cell with the inmates of a lunatic asylum. And yet the marvel was none of them ever touched him.

It seemed many minutes that the bedlam went on, then as if at a signal, they all ceased and rushed to the door. They stood there for a moment like parachutists waiting to jump from a plane, then, one after the other jumped into the wind and darkness with a wail. An awful grating sound racked the air, and sparks flew up, as each hit whatever they hit, and then they were all gone, and only the knock of the rails and the rush of wind disturbed the night.

He went to the carriage door and looked out back the way the train was coming from He held his face as far out as he could against the freezing blast of air as the train cut through the night, but he could see nothing.

Shortly after the train pulled into his station.

He had never been so glad to reach his destination. He ran up the steps and made a brisk way home through the night.

The next day he could not believe it had really happened. Maybe he had fallen asleep on the train and dreamt it. But who really confuses dreams with reality? That was the stuff of fiction.

It happened he had occasion some few days later, in daylight this time, to pass by the station again. He went and looked for the inscription on the wall to verify he hadn't dreamt it. It was there, but someone had crossed out "GRILS" and substituted "GIRLS".

But then the next morning in a spidery, appealing, pathetic script there appeared beneath it the plea:

"BUT WHAT ABOUT US POOR GRILS?"

THE PAINTING

"What, no gumtrees?"

The speaker was a pugnacious-faced, stoutly-built man, with a can of beer in one hand and he was looking over the shoulder of his diminutive, slim wife as she carefully applied oil paint in tiny dabs onto a canvas, where a picture was slowly taking shape. It was an English country scene, in fact copied from a John Constable painting, so she could lay no claim to originality. It was about 3 feet by 2 feet in size, and she had been working on it for weeks.

She looked around and smiled up at him,.

"It's a beautiful English scene, Look" she pointed towards the middle of the painting. "It's just evening, the hay wain is making its way home over the hills, creaking and rattling down the winding country lanes, the children are playing in the fields, the dog is stretching itself lazily, the sun is going down, the beautiful old trees are casting longer shadows, the little trail of smoke is rising from the chimney of the thatched cottage in the distance because it is just getting a bit chilly and they've lit a log fire, the mother-bird is circling the big tree towards her nest, the little fish and the newts and tadpoles are darting back and forth in the brook where it babbles over the stones it has babbled over for centuries, the cows are lying down to sleep in the meadows, among those trees in the forest, though you can't see them, the hedgehogs and badgers and field mice are making their way back to their nests and cosy burrows, pretty butterflies of all colours are flitting in and out among the leaves, in the farmhouse up in the distance the farmer's wife has a big stew of chicken and potatoes and vegetables from their own cottage-garden cooking away over the fire because all her sons and the farmhands will be hungry when they come home after a hard day's work, the trees in the meadow are bending with apples and apricots and pears and crabapples waiting to be picked, the hedges are laden with juicy blackberries and raspberries, the air is full of the scent of blossoms falling, and of the flowers and the honey-bees are buzzing,, ..."

'Ahhhgghh, if it hasn't got gum trees or naked women I'm not interested". He snorted gruffly and aggressively, turning away.

"Isn't my dinner ready yet?" he added with a fierce tone of voice, turning back towards her. He stood over her threateningly. "Have you been sitting slaving away with that paint all afternoon when you're supposed to be cooking my dinner?"

She shuddered and said plaintively "I've only got to put the soup on then it'll be ready". When she spoke it was with a faint, apologetic voice that you had to struggle to hear.

"Arrrgh!. You'd be sitting in front of that picture slapping that paint on all day and let me starve if I let you! I'm having another beer! If my dinner isn't ready in two minutes……. there'll be trouble!". He went noisily out of the room.

She shivered and turned away. She knew what "There'll be trouble" meant from decades of experience. She looked sadly at the painting, hating to leave it, and then down at the John Constable print she was copying.

"It looks so much like the country round where I was born" she mused softly. "I feel I know that very road. I feel I'd know my way over all those hills and down every winding lane if I had to. I feel like I know every tree, every bush, every animal, and the man driving the haywain, and the little children playing, I feel if I walked in the front door of that thatched cottage all the people there would stand up and greet me and make me welcome."

"You ought to know what's in that picture! You've been working on it for long enough!" he yelled from the kitchen, having heard her..

She looked back at the canvas. "Why, I feel I could just step into that picture and disappear…."

"Urgggh! That'd be no loss to anyone!"

He was stuffing some food into his mouth off the table. Then he came back out of the kitchen and glared at the picture some more.

"What's that big empty blob in the middle of the picture where there's no paint?" he inquired roughly.

She looked up at him dreamily and blinked slowly. "Well, I haven't finished the painting yet."

"That space has been there for days, while you just paint round it. Why are you leaving that bit blank?"

He stared it at it as if he was suddenly a great art-lover and objected to things not being done just right.

"Well, I'm leaving that bit because something special's got to go there" she said dreamily. "I have to get all the rest of the picture right first before I fill in that last, little bit."

"Stick a naked woman there and it'll be worth looking at" he said decisively as he turned away. "But a real woman, not an old bag of bones like you! Who'd want to see you with nothing on?"

Even after all the years of hearing gibes like that she couldn't help her face sagging and looking hurt and crestfallen.

It wasn't long after they got married she learned what to say to him and what not to say to him, He was very unhappy at his work, and when he came home one day she asked brightly, trying to make conversation "And how was your day, dear?" She thought that was what wives were supposed to say to their husbands.

He had just muttered something incoherent and bent his head over his dinner. She was too naïve that to know that that meant he didn't want to talk about it. She had never imagined a husband and wife wouldn't talk about things.

"Come on, how was it?" she insisted, innocently.

Irritably he muttered "This new foreman we've got….. I can't stand him! I just can't stand him!" He stamped his fist on the table so hard all the plates and cutlery on it rattled, and yelled,, his voice rising in intensity with every word, as if the words had been bottled up inside him under pressure.

"He's probably a very nice man! You should just get to know him better!" she quipped, thinking herself very smart.

She thought it was a harmless comment.

But it seemed to strike a nerve.

Smash!

He had stood up and hit her with all his might right in the face. She collapsed into a chair with blood coming out the side of her mouth. He didn't look at her or even express regret or any interest in how badly he had hurt her, but simply stamped out of the house slamming the door behind him and went down the pub. He returned very badly drunk after ten o'clock. She spent the whole evening sobbing in shock and stopping the bleeding from her cheek where her tooth had cut into her mouth with the impact. She was in a state of shock hardly believing that such a thing could happen to her. She had heard of such things indirectly, but had grown up in a household where hardly even a voice was ever raised in anger.

From then on she gathered he hated being asked anything about his day.

But he then found other reasons to bash her. If the slightest thing went wrong in the house, if he dropped a plate on the floor and broke it, or if he was putting a shelf and accidentally hit his finger with the hammer, if it rained when he wanted to go and play golf, if something was mislaid, he would glare at her and say "That was your fault": and belt her across the face. One night he belted her so hard she fell and spent all night lying on the floor in the kitchen, crying, too broken to move. She was too sore and bruised from the punchings and kickings and too humiliated even to stand up, She had still been there when he had come into the kitchen to get his breakfast in the morning, He had totally ignored her, stepped over her in fact, got himself something to eat, and walked out the door as if she was not there.

She thought once she had an argument to put to him that would cinvince him to leave her alone. She said once

"Do you...do you....do you think I'm pretty?'

He had just looked at her with a sneer on his face, looked away and grunted.

"It's just that...you things you do to me....they leave my face with bruises...and I thought...if my face has bruises...I wouldn't be as pretty...not that I'm saying I was pretty...but if you thought I was pretty...I wouldn't be pretty if you gave me bruises...so I thought...maybe you shouldn't hit me...then I wouldn't get bruises....and I would be pretty for you...."

He gave her a sour look."You were never pretty in the first place". Then he got up, walked over, and punched her just to prove his point.

She never tried that argument again.

Another time he got so mad at her over a trivial incident he had dragged her out into the garden and tied her to the clothesline by her hair. Only when it got dark had he come out and freed her, and not even by untying her but by roughly cutting her hair free with a knife.

But worse than that was when he had dragged her outside and pushed her under the house and locked her in the space there which was sealed by a small padlocked door. He had left her there like a disobedient dog until she "apologised" for serving him up for dinner something he had said he never wanted again.

He would have tied her to the bumper bar of his car when it was parked in the driveway and driven off with her once if he had not thought better of it when someone came walking by. He had intended to move the car at just over walking pace so she would have to break into a slow run to avoid falling and being dragged along until she apologised for not having his dinner ready when he had come home earlier than expected.

The worst thing he ever did was when she fled from his clutches and very inadvisedly shut herself in the garden shed. She could lock it from the inside and she thought, apart from his breaking in, she would be safe from him until his temper subsided. Unfortunately it was a drought and summer and the grass around was very dry. He had driven down to the service station, bought a can of petrol, spread petrol around the grass at the outside of the shed, watered the grass a foot away from the shed so the fire wouldn't spread, soaked the grass around the perimeter with petrol and set fire to the petrol-soaked grass. The shed was corrugated iron so there was no danger it would burn, but with flames all around the outside the shed became like an oven. It wasn't long before she started screaming. He yelled "Come out or I'll cook you like a chicken" Eventually the door opened and she came out, stumbling and covered with sweat. And edging away from him with fear on her face. What would he do now she was out? But he was laughing so much he didn't do anything. "Do that again and I'll cook you like a chicken!" was all he yelled, between his guffaws.

She learnt never to pass a negative comment on anything he did. Once when he had painted a room, she remarked that it had looked better before he painted it. He had simply upended the large can of paint of her head and walked away with a grim face as if nothing had happened out of the ordinary. It took her weeks to get the paint completely off her face and out of her hair. Of course, she had to cut her hair as short as possible as well to get the paint out. After that she came up with the idea of keeping her hair cropped short almost like someone in an infirmary who had had some terrible disease, as the shorter it was the harder it would be to pull her around by it, and it would be virtually impossible to tie her to anything by her hair. It also meant it would be less effort to clean her hair if her ever poured paint over her again.

She said to herself when she came up with that idea "Oh, you are a clever girl!"

That gave her another brainstorm – she would henceforth only wear tightfitting clothes, with nothing loose that was easy to grab onto when he got mad at her. Sometimes when he made a grab for her in a rage she found if she could stay out of his way five minutes or so he would forget that he had wanted to grab hold of her.

She often had to wear long sleeves even in the summer time to cover up the bruises he had given her, and she wore slacks to cover up the bruises on her legs. But her face she could never cover up, beyond a high collar, sunglasses and a hat with a big brim. She ran out of excuses to tell the neighbours as to why she had bruises and cuts on her face to such an extent that she had to recycle the excuses and hope they didn't notice.

"Dear" one once said to her." Are you unsteady on your feet? You seem to fall over a lot. Don't you think you should see a doctor? It could be low blood pressure, you know."

He had long ago knocked all her teeth out, not at once but with a succession of bashings over the years. But she only put her false teeth in to eat with, just in case he was to hit her and break the plate if she had them in.

After one particular beating he had given her that had out her in hospital, she had learnt after the damage he had done to her, she could never have children.

That saddened her greatly, but then, in another way, she was thankful because what on earth would he have done to children if he did have them?

He had smoked like a chimney from the time she met him, yet she had never so much as had a cigarette between her lips. She hated the smell of cigarette smoke. and she was repulsed by the stench of stale tobacco in the air and on her clothes. The smoke made her eyes smart and gave her asthma. In her fantasy she had hoped she could wean him off it after they married. Less than a week after they married she plucked up the courage to remark brightly to him across the breakfast table as he blew the smoke across the room like a belching dragon

"You know, you could make that a New Year's resolution this year – to give up smoking!"

Without saying anything, or even looking her in the eyes, he had stood up, curled one side of his lip in a scornful sneer, walked around to her side of the table and stubbed the lighted cigarette out against her cheek Then he had walked out the door

She still had a small scar there to this day.

And woe-betide her if ever he had told her to pick up a carton for him when she did the shopping and it wasn't there when she came home!

And he drank, but she didn't. When she first told him she didn't like it, he had grabbed her head, pulled it back, squeezed her nose with one hand so she had to open her mouth to breathe, and forced it into her mouth. She had to swallow a bit, but dribbled the rest out like a child refusing to take its medicine. When he had seen she had been forced to swallow a bit, he let her go.

"If I drink, you drink" he pronounced grimly. "No-one in this house is going to say they don't drink"

The strange thing was, he never tried to force her to drink again. Obviously it had occurred, even to his simple mind, that anything she drank would mean there was less for him. He had only wanted to prove, as usual, he had the power to make her do whatever he wanted.

In the same way he forced her to watch pornographic movies. When he had first put one on she had screamed "I don't want to see that! I don't want to see that!" but he had grabbed her and held her in front of the television set and forced her to look in the direction of the screen. When she tried to close her eyes, he forced them open. She screamed and struggled but the way he was pulling her eyes open she had to watch, even if only for ten seconds, then he pushed her aside. He had proved again he could make her do whatever he wanted. She walked away sobbing. All he said was, not even looking at her, sneering, indicating the woman in the film "Why don't you look like that?"

Whenever he wanted to "have his way with her" what she wanted was immaterial – he would simply rape her. She got so she saved herself actual physical violence by giving up refusing him and just putting up with it.

Whenever they were out together he would simply ignore her presence, she was just there, like a piece of furniture, and she just followed him around dutifully like a dog on an invisible lead.

He liked to have his mates round to barbecues and drinking sessions in the back garden. He would hold forth with the most foul-mouthed observations about women both in general and in particular, mentioning certain women they all knew, what they considered their most important physical attributes, and, swearing at every second word, what he would like to do to them. While he talked like this his mates would very slightly frown, and nod their heads imperceptibly towards his wife, who sat through it all with a kind of fixed smile on her face as if she didn't understand the language, as if to say "Steady on, the wife's here, you know", but it wouldn't deter him.

Occasionally he would look at her with an aggressive expression and say bluntly "Get me another drink".

When his mates came to leave they would always be excessively polite to her and grip her hands in theirs and smile knowingly at her, as if to say, "We're sorry you have to put up with all this,. But he's not a bad bloke, really, underneath it all, you know! He's really, not a bad bloke!"

It almost seemed as if he was trying to prove something by subduing her, to prove his own strength, to prove he was master of the house, to prove that no-one could challenge his status,

As the years had worn on, and she retreated into a little silent cocoon of her own, and never spoke a word out of place, as he aged, and the domineering impulse in him became less, the bashings became less frequent. But she was still not spared. As the bashings and thumpings lessened, plain verbal abuse, sarcasm, cruel put downs and sour indifference took their place.

She actually had been quite pretty in a plain sort of way when they married, but he was even then a very ugly man. His looks were as ugly as his personality. He had an ugly, asymmetrical, bony, brutish face. It was a face that always looked as if it had a grudge against the world and wanted to pick a fight with you. His body had an ugly shape – he was slightly stooped, and his stomach stuck out, His legs were ugly. Even his hands and arms were ugly. Over the years, he had got even uglier. When he spoke, his voice was ugly – it was Harsh and grating.

She took up hobbies to distract herself from the hell that was married life, but she tired of all of them. Sewing, knitting, pottery, leatherwork. jigsaw puzzles, – they distracted her for a while, but them she found the concentration seemed to numb her brain.

Then one day she discovered painting. She wasn't very good at it to start with but for some reason she found it unbelievably relaxing, just the act of transferring paint from the tubes to the paper, and seeing a picture gradually form, according to what was in her mind, and then having a change of plan and altering the final product according to some whim that came to her, it soothed her spirit, and time seemed to stand still while she was in front of a painting.. Sometimes she would sit for an hour just debating where to put the brush stroke next, but it didn't seem like wasted time.

She gradually became better at it, not only in the quality of the final product but in the technique of controlling the brush, of mixing colours and forming perfect shapes. He frankly ignored her efforts, except to make some offensive jibe at her ability to produce anything that looked like what it was supposed to represent. Except once, when she had done a self-portrait, he had cut the picture of the head of a monkey out of a book, and pasted it over her head for all to see. Oh, how he had laughed when he had seen the final product! It looked funnier than he had expected!

Then on another self portrait he had cut the nude body of a model out of a pornographic magazine and stuck it over hers, with equal hilarity. Of course, she hadn't dared to remove his vandalism, because she knew only too well what would happen to her if she did, She had simply borne the humiliation and gone on to her next project.

Then she discovered the most satisfying thing was to copy a picture she liked by a great painter out of a book. It saved the trouble of thinking up a subject yourself. She discovered the grid system by which you divided the original into squares, marked equivalent much larger squares on the canvas and then copied each square one at a time. By this means you could make a picture as many times bigger than the one you were copying as you liked. She liked a picture about 3 feet by 2 feet, because it was just small enough to pick up, and to work on from a seated position, and to take in all at once, but big enough to really look like something.

That was how she came to be doing the John Constable picture.

Everything in it reminded her of the place where she came from. The rural scene was so different to the world around her now. The land was green and fecund and fertile, not dry and dusty and full of drab colours. The people were soft, and gentle, and peaceful and polite.

Then the day after he had made the jibe about the big empty blob in the middle of the picture, he came home and she was gone.

He figured at first she must have slipped out to buy something extra for dinner, but the shops were a long way away. It wasn't like her, and the shopping trolley was in its usual place. Her sunglasses which she wore to cover up the bruises round her eyes were still on the dining room table. The coat she wore when she went out to cover the bruises on her arms was still on the back of the chair. Maybe she had fallen sick and been taken away in an ambulance, but surely they would have left a note, he thought.

He looked at the painting. It was actually finished. The blank "blob" in the middle was gone. In its place was a lady in a bonnet, a lacy blouse and a long, flowing, beautifully embroidered skirt holding a basket of flowers under her arm. There were flowers along the side of the trail she was walking down, and it looked as if she had been picking them. She was walking past the haywain and the children and the dog that was stretching itself, probably going home to be home before the sun was finally set, but she looked so relaxed and happy she wouldn't be adverse to stooping down and picking a few more flowers if she saw some that took her fancy. She was looking straight out of the picture, instead of the way she was going, and because, of course, the picture was two dimensional, wherever you stood in front of the picture the eyes seemed to be looking straight at you. The hand of the arm that was not holding the basket was raised just to the level of her head and she was giving a quiet wave with it, to whoever she was looking at, but because her eyes were looking straight out of the picture she seemed to be waving at you. Her face bore an enigmatic, all-knowing smile of radiant peace.

"Well, she finished the picture before she shot through!" he said to himself. Then he kept staring at the picture. Something about the shape of the woman's body and the way she was walking, for the way people walk is as characteristic as a signature, made him frown. Then he snatched the picture off the easel and held it closer, because it was more than the way the woman was walking that looked familiar. He looked keenly at the figure of the woman, who seemed to be looking straight at him, smiling, and waving to him. He held it closer so the painting was almost touching his nose. There was something about the way she was walking, and the dress she was wearing, and the way she was holding her arm…. and her face…….. He looked closer at her face.. and closer.. and closer…

He slammed the picture back onto the easel, and went to a drawer for a magnifying glass. He held it right up to the face of the woman so he could see it better, and studied it intently. No, it couldn't be!

He paced around the room in a circle for some minutes like a caged animal, slamming his right fist into his left hand, swearing, and breathing deeply.

Then an enlarged photograph of his football team he had had taken and had blown up and framed hanging on the wall caught his eye. Something occurred to him.

That photograph had been enlarged from a small snap he had taken. The photographer who enlarged it had equipment with which you could being an original up on the screen, and enlarge it to the size you want depending on the quality of the original and the detail you wanted to show. He grabbed a telephone book and started searching madly for his number.

He got him on the phone. The photographer was nonplussed at being rung at such an hour. The husband spoke frantically.

"You the guy that blows up pictures? You the guy that blew up that football picture for us?"

"Do you know what time it is?" was the only answer he got. "It's ten o'clock at night? Who are you?"

"It doesn't matter who I am. You blew up a picture for me once. I want another one done!"

"Well, come round at ten o'clock tomorrow morning. And maybe I'll do it!"

"I want it done now.! I'll pay you whatever you want!" And then, because he sensed the slamming down of a phone would be the next thing he would hear, he spluttered out "It's a matter of life and death!".

The photographer gave an exasperated sigh and inquired in a tired voice "How can it be a matter of life and death?"

The husband thought quickly. What could he say? "My wife's disappeared. ...Something's happened to her....." Well, he was only telling the truth. Then he blurted out again "It's a matter of life and death...... I've got a picture here....it's a painting she was doing....You know that equipment you've got.... I want you to blow it up.... Like you did with my team shot... I want you to blow it up as big as you can ....so I can see the detail. It may have a clue to where she's gone.......There's no time to lose.."

After a lot more badgering the photographer relented and said he could come round and bring the picture.

When the photographer opened his front door the frantic husband barged in like a raging bull, the painting under his arm. "I want you to blow this up, this part right in the middle there, with the woman. I want you to blow it up so I can see her face more clearly. I want you to magnify it as much as you can!"

The photographer had never had such a strange request before.

"But it's not a photograph, it's a painting. If you magnify it, all you'll see is brush strokes. And the more you magnify it, you'll just see bigger brush strokes. The more you magnify it, the less it will look like anything!"

"I don't care. I want you to blow it up!"

The photographer was frankly afraid of the physical presence of the enraged husband, and figured the sooner he complied with his bizarre request and got him out of the house the better. He turned on his equipment and put the large painting under the magnifier. An image of the picture came up on the screen He turned handles and adjusted lenses so it became bigger and bigger. He focussed down on the face of the woman.

The photographer's demeanor changed from one of irritation, anger and fear to one of professional amazement. "This is incredible!" he exclaimed, "The more I magnify it, the more detail you can see. There no brush strokes. It's just like a photograph.... A photograph with unbelievably fine detail."

"But...it's not a photograph. It's a painting! The wife was doing it! She's been doing it for months! There was a big blob missing in the centre, and now it's been painted in, but she's disappeared!"

He spoke like he was at the end of his tether, and waved his ugly arms in the air.

"I don't know anything about that" the photographer said. "All I see when I blow it up is finer and finer detail. Look!"

The frantic husband looked through the viewer. His jaw sagged. There was the smiling face, looking straight at him, in the flowery bonnet and the delicate white lace collar. There was not a trace of worry, or care or even wrinkles on the face. It was not the face that had looked across the breakfast table that morning, but it was the young, sweet, innocent, carefree face he had married, but with a look in it now that betokened added years of wisdom, and all-knowing. It looked like a face that had freed itself of all the worries of the world, and was now living in a serene paradise.

And that face was the face of his wife. Now he knew where she had gone,

She had painted herself into the picture.

THE GOOD
SAMARITANS

"Bitte! Bitte! Oh, bitte! Helfst du mich! Oh bitte! Ich habe Gefahr…Oh, bitte!"

"What's that? It's a man's voice, coming from over the edge. What's he saying?"

"He's calling for help. It must be another hiker who's come to grief and fallen over the edge. Come and look".

The year was 1919. The place was Austria. The speakers were two fresh-faced young Britons, a man and a woman, on a walking tour. They were both disgustingly healthy-looking, with pale legs, knobbly knees, shorts and big hiking boots. They were descending a steep mountain trail that had a perilous drop to one side and a towering rock face one the other when they had heard the cry of distress.

Now they rushed to the edge and looked over. About twenty feet down a young man in hiking clothes like themselves was literally hanging by his fingers to a rock ledge. His legs dangled and waved hysterically in the air as he vainly tried to get a toe-hold on the cliff face.

"Oh! The poor fellow. He's hanging on for dear life! He must have been climbing down the cliff and slipped. He can't stay like that much longer! He'll go! I'll have to go down!"

The woman looked at him in horror.

"But Paul you can't go down. There's no footholds. You're not a climber. We haven't even got a rope! We have to go and get help!"

"I tell you there's no time. He's hanging by his fingers. He can't last much longer. I'll have to go down. If I can get beneath him I can push him in towards the cliff so he can get a foothold. It's the only way. there are footholds if you can just find them."

"But Paul you'll end up like him. You can't, Paul, you just can't risk it! You can't put your own life in danger just to save his! Well go and get help".

"Oh, bitte! Bitte!....."

"There's not time! I keep telling you that. I can't just leave him without trying. It's his only chance!"

The young man dropped himself to the ground, and edged himself backwards over the cliff. The girl was right. It looked like a hopeless exercise, even for a proper climber, which he was not. Little stones and clumps of dirt started to plummet to the valley below. He was spread-eagled against the wall of the cliff, each hand clinging to what it could, each foot thrust against what support it could find. His limbs were trembling and his muscles already seemed like jelly, and still fifteen feet above the Austrian man.

The Austrian moaned. "Oh, schnell, schnell, bitte……"

The British boy hung over a protruding tree branch with his left arm. His right hand clung to a wedge of rock. His left foot was in a crevice, his right foot probed for support. He looked down. Yes, if he get his foot onto that piece of rock- it looked strong enough to take his weight- he could then manoeuvre himself lower. he stretched his toes like a ballet dancer until he touched it, then he gradually slid his arm from over the branch, putting more of his weight on his right foot. It held. Now he held the branch with just his hand. He had gained about eighteen inches. he looked down to his left and saw a tuft of foliage that looked like it might take his weight. If he could transfer his mass to it he could then let go with his right hand and descended still further. He pressed on it gingerly. It felt firm, so he gradually put more of his weight upon it. Suddenly it gave way and in terror he clutched the rock he was just letting go of. He had nearly fallen. He stayed absolutely still for many seconds, collecting his senses, and steadying his nerves. Then he saw the foliage that had given way obscured a stump of a branch that held much more promise of supporting his weight, if he could go just six inches more to the left. He edged his weight towards it, and once again shifted more and more of his balance onto it. This time it held. He was nearer to the Austrian man. It seemed to him his best plan would be to make for the ledge that was below him and to the left. From there he would have a firm base from which to push up and support him so he get a foothold to climb up, although the ledge was too far from the Austrian man for him to just drop onto it. A few more manoeuvres and he achieved this destination. How good it felt to feel something solid beneath him again. His wife watched him over the edge. She looked a long way above him. It seemed remarkable he had come so far. Now he reached up to the right and grabbed the Austrian's foot. He pushed it upwards. "Push, man, push" he shouted. "Put your weight on my hand and raise yourself upwards. Push, I can take the weight!"

The Austrian man pushed. The Englishman could feel his leg trembling in his hand. With a great effort the man raised himself until he could hook his body over the branch he had heretofore just clung to. "Now climb, man, climb" the Englishman urged him.

The Austrian got a foothold and painfully raised himself even further, until he had one knee on the branch, then both knees, then he was standing, clinging to rocks above him with his hands. The Englishman then started up towards him, until he could actually take the Austrian's foot and actually place it in toeholds. He put his hand under the Austrian's backside and gave him the final leverage for his last manoeuvre that took him to top. Then in a flurry of sighs and grunt of strain and pathetic exclamations the Austrian was over and in safety. He collapsed on the ground clutching his arms in his hands as if he was afraid they had really broken off.

The Englishman's head appeared over the edge. Suddenly the acute tension that had given him the strength and will power to perform the feat had gone out of him. He felt weak, but he was on the home stretch. He grabbed a rock to pull himself up over the edge. His head and shoulders appeared, then

"Aaaaargh...!"

The rock came loose.

He fell.

His wife screamed and buried her head in her hands. Then she looked in horror over the edge. By a thousand to one chance, there he was, hanging by his jacket on a branch. His legs and arms waved helplessly like a spider hanging from a web. He made frantic efforts to twist himself upwards so he could grab the branch like a bat or sloth, but every movement he made engendered a tearing sound as his jacket gave way a little more. He was looking death in the face, when

"Hold on! Hold on! We have rope!" Another party of climbers had arrived on the scene, and a brawny German was looking over the edge. They had already fastened one end of a strong rope to a hefty tree, and now he was coming down. He reached the imperilled and brave Englishman and took him in his arms, from where the pulling power of four men above was sufficient to raise the both of them to safety. But the Englishman was beside himself. The strain of the first rescue, the physical extremes he had put himself to, then the sudden plunge almost to the jaws of death, and the unexpected rescue, were too much for him, and he lay shivering and blubbering in the grass. His wife leant over him hugging him.

It was twenty minutes later. Her husband had recovered. The Austrian men was in agitated conversation with the Germans who had so fortuitously arrived on the scene with their rope. She herself had something she wanted to say to the man her husband had saved. She was annoyed that he had not yet come over to her husband to thank him. She went over to where he was standing with the Germans.

She was still very shaken. Her voice trembled when she spoke. She held her hair back against the strong wind and looked keenly into the man's face. "My husband risked his life for you, you know". She said it in a tone as if she expected some rejoinder. He shrugged and lifted one side of his mouth. "So? I did not ask him."

"He said he couldn't leave you there!"

"Zat is right. It vas his duty. But I did not ask him. There is no shame to lose your life in doing duty. Himmel! I haf never been so near death! In all my time in der war, I vas not so near to mein death….."

Her husband had now recovered enough to stand up, and he came limping over, his hand extended. "We are pleased to help you. We are Christians on a tour across the whole of Europe. We are only students, so we do not have the wherewithal to travel in style, so we spend a lot of time "slogging it", but we see more of the country that way, and meet more of the people. Especially those falling over cliffs, heh?" He gave the Austrian an ingenuous, toothy smile. The Austrian man made a peculiar twitch of his head in agreement.

"Zat is good. All young people should spend some time to see Europe, the home of civilization. The open air, the country, the mountains, simple living, climbing, hiking, valking, it is gut. Der government should pay students a vage so zey can travel".

He annoyed her so much with his lack of gratitude she went over to the party of Germans who were preparing to go. Her husband stayed talking to him for a while, then joined her. He noticed her displeasure.

She rested her arm on his shoulder. "You know, I am so proud of you. You risked your life to save someone else. That man owes his life to you. If it wasn't for you he'd be a body smashed to pieces at the bottom of that ravine, and in years to come, his friends and family would have said when his name came up "Oh, so-and-so. He was killed when still a young man, in a climbing accident in the alps. It was very sad.' Just like bringing a baby into the world, you've given life to another. Whatever that man does from now on, the world can thank you for. Why, you might have saved the life of a great humanitarian".

"You know" said her husband "what you say is true. I can't deny that I feel somewhat proud of what I did. But, you know, when you said 'Don't go down there, you can't save him', and I insisted, I actually agreed with you. I really thought I was a goner when I went over the edge. Often when you're undertaking a perilous task, you feel something inside you that tells you can make it, and sometimes it tells you you can't, instinctively, so you hold back. But this time I really thought it was a hopeless task. I thought you were going to be left up there alone. But I was too afraid not to. Everyone would have said, those who were not there, 'Why didn't you try and save him', and I couldn't have taken the humiliation. I was more afraid of that than of falling. and yet I was afraid of falling. crazy, isn't it. Oh yes, it would have been so easy to have left him".

"I must say he didn't seem particularly grateful" said the wife "He was grateful to be alive but not grateful to you for saving him. He didn't seem particularly aware that you had risked your life for him. He almost seemed to think it was no more than your duty. He was all for courage and sacrifice but he didn't strike me as a brave man himself".

"Well, I'd say he was a typical German, if you don't mind my saying so".

"You know, he didn't even tell us his name".

"No. Wait, he did tell me his name, while I was talking to him back there. It was a funny name. It sounded like the name of a country bumpkin, but his first name sounded like something French. That's right, I remember him saying, he was changing his surname to a much more common-sounding German name.

"So what was the name then of this young man you could have let die yet risked your own life to snatch from the very jaws of death?"

"His name was - Adolphe Hitler".

THE LAST WALTZ

"So it's all agreed, it's your turn, Steve, to ask the ugliest girl at the dance for a waltz!"

Steve winced. "Oh, do I really have to? Can't I do something else, like drink a cup of dishwater or something. Ugly women just turn me right off!"

"Steve, that was agreed when you joined the Seven Club each of the seven of us once every seven days would take turns to do something repellent, drawn out of a hat, out of seven repellent choices, and tonight you're the one, and you drew the option of asking the ugliest girl at the dance for a waltz."

"But ugly women turn me right off! I've got an aversion to them. I think the first day I was born I must have been scared by an ugly nurse. Can't we make an exception just in this one case? Can't someone else do it, and I'll agree to do three repellent things instead next week?"

"Steve, you know that's against the rules of the club. If you refuse one obligation, you're out, and you'll forego forever all the benefits of being in the club!"

Steve made a gruesome face for about a quarter of a minute, then finally lowered his head and nodded."All right, I'll do it!"

Then he added as an afterthought "I just hope she isn't fat as well!"

She had a hare lip, a broken nose, her ears stuck out, her eyebrows met over her nose, and she weighed nineteen stone. Every week for six years she had been coming to the dance, but she had never once been asked by a man to get up on the floor with him. The only exception was the barn dance where you pass from one partner to another after each turn so the man who asks you up knows he will not be stuck with you.

Apart from that she sat there like a statue watching the couples whirling past number after number. Her face was blank so no-one could know the pain behind it, but each Friday night that she sat there was just ache and suffering for her. People wondered why she kept coming, but it was simply a case of hope springing eternal and never being vanquished by reason. Always the idea was in her mind that tonight it would be different. But always at the end of the evening she would pick her things up and go home heartbroken. She was surrounded by beauty, but it made her sad. How could that be? The final result of beauty, was sadness. That paradox perplexed her.

What was this weekly function that she always came to? It was held in old Pasquale's "Silver Ballroom", an incredibly chintzy, gaudy, tasteless and pretentious cavernous reception hall, where facades, false ceilings and a bar had been thrown together from masonite, plastic, cardboard, chipboard and polyurethane foam so that, with cunning lighting at the right angles, it actually looked like something glamorous. if you didn't look too closely.

Pasquale himself who owned the building and half the other buildings in the street, didn't know one dance step from another. Originally the dance had been run by someone else who only rented his hall for the night, but when Pasquale realised that this person could pay his exhorbitant rent and still make a profit on the takings, he got the idea of running the dance himself and getting the takings instead of the rent which were obviously bigger. He hired a few professional dance instructors to play the records and call the dances, and just sat in the doorway with a self-satisfied look collecting the money and watching the dancers, who to his eyes were like dollar signs going round and round on a poker machine dial. Every week he looked more genial, more well-fed, more plump, more affluent, more well-oiled, as if he was eating his money.

The decor of the place was bright, but pretty tasteless. There was only one genuine article that wasn't bodgied up in the whole place, and that was Pasquale's nine wonderful chandeliers.

Those chandeliers! They weighed so much it had taken four men to lift each one into place. He had encountered them at auction one day, and taken a fancy to them, awed by their gruesome presence, their uniqueness, and their utter impracticality, which was so obvious he thought they must be a valuable item. He said "I got to have them for my ballroom". Twenty-five bulbs each one took. Although he had got them for a song (he wouldn't have bought them otherwise), he has winced at the thought of what keeping all those bulbs functional would cost him. He had had them hung on the thickest chains he could find where he thought they would make the most impression, three across one end, three across the other end and three across the middle of the hall. The tradesmen who had hung them told him the beams were not really strong enough to take the weight, but he had insisted anyhow. Everything was for appearance, the look of the place was everything, nothing else mattered.

Because she had a strange sort of superstition about it, as if it would one day bring her luck, she always sat right under the chandelier that was in the middle of one end of the hall.

A waltz was called for. Swiftly, one by one, the girls rose from their seats around the walls as men came up and asked them to dance. Soon there were only a few left sitting, and some little groups who just then wanted to talk rather than dance. Beautifully groomed men walked this way and that past her to collect their partners, but gave her only a passing glance then a quick look away as they hurried to take the hand of the one they had chosen. The floor was a dizzying whirl of dancers swirling round like the waters of a stream turned by a gigantic hand. Skirts whirled and black shoes shone and lithe bodies flitted athletically. It was all glitter, glitter, excitement and glamour. And she could not be part of it, She sat and ached. The music wailed and droned....

"May I have this dance?"

A very good-looking young man had stepped up to her and was holding his hand towards her and smiling. She just stared at him and blinked, she couldn't believe he was talking to her. Then, simultaneously, above the music she heard a roar like a clap of thunder, and looked up instinctively, and had at once an impression of myriads of light beams coming towards her like snow, and stars, shining and glittering and sparkling so bright she had to close her eyes ....

But then the handsome young took her hand gently and she found herself rising up at his bidding as lightly as Pavlova. She usually had to steady herself with one hand to manage her weight when she got out of a chair, but this time she seemed to rise to her feet as if she had no weight at all. And all the time, though she could see him perfectly clearly, he looked so handsome, and she was so surprised, that there were stars, stars, stars in her eyes.

He put one hand behind her back, and with the other held her arm high, and she found herself being swirled around the floor as easily as a feather in the wind. She had danced so little over the six years she had been coming there, she was afraid she would fumble the steps, in fact she always did fumble the steps when she tried them by herself, but now, with just the slightest inclination through the body contact this way and that, her feet (those great clumsy feet) seemed to fall exactly into the right place, like a concert pianist's fingers flitting precisely over the right notes. And all the time he was talking softly into her ear, telling her how he had seen her week after week and thought how beautiful he was but never before been courageous enough to ask her to dance.

She felt so light on her feet and seemed to be doing everything so right, she suddenly had a great desire to know what she looked like dancing with this man. The walls were all mirrored, so she glanced away from his face to catch a glimpse of herself, not from vanity (what a thought!) but from desperate curiosity. The mirrors reflected the rapidly whirling and swayingfigures of all the dancers, and it was hard to pick out any single couple, the reflections changed so quickly. Now and then she thought she could see the image of her partner, but then she could tell it must be not so, because it was not her he was dancing with, it was a beautifully slim and elegant girl in a fabulous dress. There must be someone almost his double on the floor. But still whenever she looked it persisted, she was sure she could see the reflection of her partner, but not her. He looked as if he were dancing with someone totally different. Perhaps they were moving too fast to see, and it was an illusion of angles.

Then, it seemed the other couples were one by one leaving the floor and standing round the edge and watching the couples that were left dancing. And then it seemed it was just her and her partner they were watching, and each of their faces had a look of wonderment. And then, they were the only ones left on the floor, and the waltz seemed to have been going, not just for minutes, but for hours, but she didn't feel the least tired, when she looked at the reflection, she could see her partner, but it was not her great ungainly hulk he had in his arms, it was a beautiful slim, elegant wonderfully groomed girl, in the most glittering, fantastic costume she could ever have imagined. Was it just the confusion of the movement of the lights and the mirrors? Then, she found herself forced to look down at herself, to prove to herself it was really her on the floor. But she saw not herself, but the very figure she could see in the reflection. But she knew it was herself! She had been transformed into something she always wished she could be! And now they were waltzing, waltzing, waltzing so fast and so exhilaratingly, but she did not feel the least tired, or even feel she missed the fraction of a step or the speck of timing and with their bodies together they moved as one, and the music was more beautiful than she had ever heard before, and the whole hall full of the other dancers simply stood round the edge of the dance floor and stared at them in wonder…

But then he suddenly let her go and stepped away from her, and though he was still dancing it was by himself, and he was gradually moving away from her, and when she moved towards him, no matter how fast she moved he moved away faster, though he was still dancing and he still was talking to her, "I've enjoyed it so much, you're so beautiful, you dance so beautifully, I've never danced with anyone like you ever, but I must go now, I must go now, I must go now…" and all the time the stars and lights were in her eyes, but now they were getting brighter, brighter, brighter, and now so bright she had to close her eyes and now they were burning against her but though she closed her eyes there were still lights and stars and sparkling and she could still see him but he was dancing away from her…

There were screams and shouts and everyone rushed towards her, but underneath the massive chandelier of crystal and bulbs and iron and chains where it had fallen she did not move, and looked as if it had hit her so hard she had known nothing from the moment it fell, but though blood was flowing from the great gashes in her crushed head, her chest no longer moved. Yet her eyes were still open and seemed to be looking for something far away she had known for one moment but was now lost forever.

THE MAN
ON THE RUN

I was at a country roadhouse attached to a service station early in the evening. My car had broken down but luckily there was a co-operative mechanic on duty who was prepared to stay back to fix it. He said it would take at least two hours, and the road house supplied reasonable cooked meals and I was extremely hungry I took the opportunity to sit down to a plate of fish and chips, not what I would normally eat but I was ravenous and anything looked good. It was just getting dark.

There were no other customers, but suddenly a car pulled up outside, a man about forty dressed in a dishevelled manner got out, there were some heated words exchanged between him and the driver until the driver reached over, slammed the passenger door and drove off with a scream of tyres. The passenger came into the roadhouse. In contrast to his cheap-looking clothes, he had a very intelligent face. His eyes darted round the interior of the establishment, and to the road outside, as if he was trying to make up his mind what to do next, when seeing me he made a bee-line for my table.

"I say" he accosted me, in a voice that was polite, yet at the same time earnest. "Do you mind if I sit with you?"

As I am not an unfriendly person I replied "Of course not".

He sat down, put his elbows on the table and started wringing his hands and looking at me, the roadhouse and the road outside, with jerky movements of his head.

"I just feel safer to be with someone" he explained.

Now such a statement would normally put me on my guard, because if such a fellow felt unsafe, it would make me think "Why? Was he on the run from the law? Was he a criminal on the run from other criminals? Was he a schizophrenic imagining non-existent assailants? But for some reason, I felt no no danger.

"Aren't you having something to eat?" I asked him after some minutes.

He looked into my eyes apologetically. "I'm out of money" he explained. "I'm totally skint. I can't afford anything".

As if the mention of food hade made him remember how hungry he was, his eyes drifted to my freshly fried chips, and I saw him swallow as if the sight of them made him salivate.

"Have some" I said. "I can't eat them all."

He took one quickly, and then another, and another. He wasn't exactly consuming them gluttonously, but his ravenous hunger was obvious.

"I saw you get out of a car and have some altercation with the driver. Was that a friend of yours?"

"No, I was hitchhiking. That is the extremity I have come to".

"Hitch hiking? At your age?"

"Yes. It's the only way I can get around, I have no money, and no transport. He refused to take me any further, because he didn't like what I was saying. But hitching is the only way I can get to where I have to go".

"And where do you have to go?" I asked.

He seemed to consider if he should answer, and eventually said.

"I can't tell you that"

"And where have you come from?"

"Neither can I tell you that".

He looked at me apologetically, but not shiftily.

Then his eyes wandered to the table next where a newspaper lay. He reached over and flicked through the pages, then finding the crossword page put it in front of himself and took out a pen.

"You're going to think me very rude" he said with a slight smile "but I find doing cryptic crosswords distracts me from stressful thoughts, not to mention the beneficial mental exercise. Excuse me, I'm going to do this".

Now I know these "cryptic crosswords". If I sit down for half an hour with one I may get a quarter of the clues. He filled in one space, then studied the next clue and filled in another, then another, then another. I had read that applicants for Bletchley House where they broke the codes in the war were given the Daily Telegraph cryptic crossword as a test and the record time for solving one was eleven minutes. In less than ten minutes he had finished this one. He looked at me with the hint of a smile.

"You get used to the mind processes of the fellows who put these together, and you follow their logic and it helps you to get the answer faster" he explained. "I am quite familiar with the way this fellow's mind works, so they usually are no trouble for me".

Then it occurred to me perhaps he had just written letters in at random so I said "Can I see?"

I took the page and scanned a few of the clues, and his answers, but sure enough, his answers made sense. I thought, this fellow must have the mind of gargantuan abilities, unless he had perhaps seen the answers and memorised them, but that idea was preposterous, because it was today's paper, and the answers were not published until the next day.

"I've got several university degrees, you know" he suddenly remarked.

When he said it, he didn't say it in a tone to boast, it more implied: wasn't it a sorry state of affairs that such an educated person should be reduced to the predicament he was in?

"In what fields?" I enquired. I wanted to could make up my mind if he was telling the truth.

"Arts, Law, Physics, Anthopology.." he said in an off-hand way, still looking round earnestly, as if he had more important things to think about.

"From where?" I probed further.

He told me the name of the institution in an off-hand way as if to imply "What did it matter?"

I saw a chance to trip him up, if he was lying.

"My wife worked there for many years in the administration" I said. (This of course was a lie). "She knew all the major professors and lecturers quite well. So you'd probably remember Professor John Hawkins" It was just a name I had plucked out of the air. I expected him to give me a suspicious look, narrow his eyes while he was thinking what he should say, and then reply

"Oh, yes, good old Professor Hawkins. Knew him well!" but instead he stared for a few moments into my face with a look that implied I was totally mad, and eventually said "There was never anyone there by that name."

If he was dissimulating, he was doing it well.

"Perhaps that wasn't the name "I said vaguely, not wanting him to know I had been trying to trick him, and shrugged as if my mistake should better be quickly forgotten.

Then, as if he had come to a great decision to un-burden himself, he leaned forward and looked into my eyes earnestly.

"They're after me".

I had just started to think of him as an intelligent fellow who had, not by his own fault, fallen on hard times. At these words I suddenly began to revise my opinion

"Who's 'they'?" I asked.

He stared at me with a rather impatient look, as if I should know already, then he looked away, then looked back at me as if it was time to unburden himself.

"There is a Shadow Government that controls the world" he stated, speaking slowly with great emphasis.

I do not know if I actually drew back in my seat a lit-tle at this stage, but mentally I drew back. I had heard all this before and I felt I knew almost word for word what was coming next. What surprised me was that people who carry on like this are usually non-achievers with low IQs, who have an enormous chip on their shoulder and knit this web of conspiracy to justify their own failings on the basis of "everyone is against them", and yet he was obviously not of this ilk. With such a person I might have got up and walked away, possibly with a rude rejoinder, because I hate being ear-bashed, but because this fellow had painted such an impressive picture of himself I decided to let him talk.

"Forget everything you have read in history books" he went on, "and in the papers" it is all wrong. Well, not all of it, but a large part of it. There is a Shadow Government, an unseen presence, that controls our lives. They start wars, they finish wars, they cause depressions, they cause boom times, they manipulate the media, the so-called 'Governments' of the world, the public services, the educational institutions, business…everything, are in the palm of their hands. It's all about control".

He emphasised the last word, "control", as if it were the key to everything.

"Why, there are even chemicals put the food we eat to make us more tractable that we may remain forever under their control".

"You eat it" I chipped in, indicating the empty plate of chips he had devoured. "Has your mind been therefore contaminated?"

"What choice do I have?" he came back quickly. "I cannot starve. I cannot grow my own food. I did for a while, and made sure everything that went into my lips was safe, but that was when I had money, but even as I did, there are chemicals put into the air that are absorbed by the rain and enter the food.

"It was just by chance I discovered the existence of the Shadow Government" he went on. "I happened to meet a very wise man who was near death, but before he died he imparted to me the knowledge he gleaned from years of investigation. Like me he was maligned, ridiculed, in fact driven to an early grave, but he was able to impart his knowledge to me. I was skeptical at first, so I spent years researching, reading, infiltrating, wherever I could, and came to the inescapable conclusion that everything he had told me was true".

"OK" I said, interrupting him. I had the bombshell rejoinder I always give those who rant on this way. "If these people are so powerful, why haven't they eliminated you? It should be so easy for them to do it, as you are only one, indigent individual, unarmed, unprotected, and they according to you, are so powerful."

He looked at me with a knowing smile, as if he was so used to that objection he was wondering why it had been so long coming.

"They'd like to" he answered. "But they have obviously decided it would only draw attention to my campaign. I am not an unknown person, if I was eliminated, there would be questions asked to the effect that, if I am just a lunatic, why was it necessary to eliminate me? If they did eliminate me, they would have to make it look like an accident, but even accidents will look suspicious if there is a grain of doubt... and also, they do not know how much I know, and to how many people I have imparted what I know, and how many of them have believed me....literally 'eliminating me', wiping me off the face of the Earth, which they are quite capable of doing, would destroy any chance they have of finding that out.

"Having said that..." he suddenly started wringing his hands again. "I am convinced now they have decided to finish me off. That's why I am on the run like never before. I have stepped onto buses and slipped out another door... I have slipped into public toilets, removed slats from tiny windows and climbed out the back of them, I have walked through the boarding tunnels of planes and slipped out a staff exit, I have been very hard to track, but I know they are close on my trail now...that's why, I can't linger here long.

For some reason at that moment he looked down at himself, and surveyed his own disheveled appearance.

"My family wouldn't recognize me now" he commented. "I must look like I have been made up to play the part of a tramp in some film".

"Like the fellow in 'The Man With the Twisted Lip' the Sherlock Holmes story" I remarked.

(In this story, a man incurs great losses through gambling and needs money, so having theatrical training, he makes himself up to look like a pathetic beggar with a deformed face, and sits by the side of the road begging, but finds he can make more that way than in his regular job).

His face lit up. "Oh, you are familiar with Sherlock Holmes. I know the plots like the back of my hand, I admire Conan Doyle greatly, he was a great man, with a terrific mind. Sherlock Holmes is just a fraction of his output, but even on that basis he was clearly a great man. Name any of his stories and I can tell you the plot, and name every character, and also point out a few discrepancies as regard to the truth, for there are some, he was not perfect He asserts, in "The Solitary Cyclist" for instance, that you can tell which way a bicycle is being ridden by the way the front wheel sometimes crosses over the track of the back wheel, but this is false". Also I tried to put all the stories in chronological order because, as you know, they were not written in chronological order, some of the later ones go back to the early years of the association between Watson and Holmes, and some even to before Holmes met Watson, and Dr Watson actually marries, moves away, then is widowed, moves back then marries again, but there a few references to dates and events that do not fit, so he was not perfect".

"Yes, Conan Doyle wrote 60 Sherlock Holmes stories. Four novels and 56 short stories" he continued, as if he had unfinished business with the subject. Then he looked at me with a smile and rattled off the titles of each, in the order they appeared in print. I had no way of knowing how accurate he was, but from my less familiar knowledge of the stories, I could not ascertain any fault. Then he proceeded to rattle off the name of every book of the bible.

"I have a mania for lists" he explained, with a tinge of apology in his voice. "I can't help it. But just as a mental exercise to keep the brain agile, it is a good thing." He looked forlornly away for a second. "And it is so important I keep my brain agile".

"And Conan Doyle believed in spiritualism" I chipped in.

"Spiritualism is true!" he blurted out, fixing me with the most joyous look he had exhibited since we had begun talking, as if the subject was the one thing that would divert his mind from his present predicament. "I am in constant contact with the dead, or the so-called dead. But of course, The Shadow Government would have you believe it is impossible. Conan Doyle did not just know the right way to do it, but he was smart enough to know it could be done. Why, do you think such a smart fellow would be taken in by an idea that had no basis?".

Well, this was a point I had often pondered.

"But there are people who believe in UFOs, aliens among us, yetis" I ventured. to change the subject, as I could see it was a waste of time to pursue spiritualism, But he immediately jumped in with

"UFOs have landed" he immediately responded. "There are aliens amongst us, and the yeti, I have seen it in my travels to that part of the world".

"And are these 'aliens' as dangerous as these people who are after you?" I asked, with a tinge of sarcasm.

He made a dismissive inclination of his head. "They are unimportant. They have no ill intentions towards us, and if they did, their influence pales into insignificance against the perfidy of the Shadow Government."

"Do you speak any foreign languages?" I enquired. It just suddenly struck me a fellow who was so learned might. I expected him maybe to say "a couple", three" or even "four", and was quite taken aback when he said

"Fifteen. But the only reason I learn a language is if there is a work pertaining to exposure of the Shadow Government in that language that I wish to read, for if I have to read it in translation, how do I know nuances of the original meaning might have been lost or that the translator was actually working for the Shadow Government?"

Fifteen. Now, how on earth could I test this, not knowing even one myself? Then I realized I had been overseas recently, and had in the car a pamphlet in at least a dozen languages advising travellers what to do if they lose their passport.

"Look" I said "That's just so timely. I have a scrap of documentation in a language I can't even judge as to what it is, but for a reason that would bore you I really need to know what it says. Perhaps with your wide linguistic knowledge you can translate it"

"Of course" he said.

I rushed out to my car and retrieved the pamphlet. I scanned the English text so I would have a fair idea what it was about, and selected the most obscure-looking language, tore it out and brought it to him.

"I would be very pleased if you could translate that I said. "I need to know what it says."

He looked at it. "Ah, it is in Armenian. Its alphabet has 39 characters, you know. It is a language many times removed from our own. But this is simply what to do if you lose your passport. It says ..." and he read, pretty exactly word for word what the English text had said. So, unless he knew only one foreign language, and it was Armenian, by a million to one coincidence the one I had chosen, once again he was not lying!

He looked at me then with great surprise."Why on Earth would you want a translation of that?"

"Oh, I thought it was something else. Someone left it in my letter box.. and I had a few people playing tricks on me lately..so I needed to know what it meant. Perhaps someone saw it lying on the pavement, thought it belonged to me and slipped it in my letterbox"

"Most peculiar" he commented, looking at me as if he was quite mystified by my story. I don't blame him. My efforts to prove him a liar were turning me into a mammoth liar.

"You are very afraid, aren't you" I commented for no particular reason.

Then he looked at me with a peculiar expression, as if he was deciding whether to impart a vital piece of information to me. He obviously decided he should, because he suddenly looked round, to check no-one was watching us, and opened his jacket for a split second, so I could see what he had strapped to his chest. It was a gun in a holster.

"The great equalizer" he explained with a knowing look."I intend to use it if I have to."

Then he momentarily lifted the other side of his jacket and revealed a knife in a sheath.

"Just in case the gun doesn't stop them and they get up close enough for me to use it. I'm determined if they ever get their hands on me, I'll finish off a few of them first".

So now I was alone with a desperate man who was armed and prepared to use his weapons.

Then something seemed to come to him.

"I say". He looked at me as if he was about to make a proposition he was not sure about. He put his hand inside his coat and started to remove a bundle of papers. "You seem to be an open-minded fellow, and intelligent, can I give you a summary of my treatise, it is a cut down version, the entirety will run to volumes, but I would like you to have this, and if anything happens to me...."

He had half taken it out, when there was a shout from the mechanic.

"Ready!" was what the laconic fellow screamed out.

I wanted to have the document, I wanted to understand this fellow more, however I said "I'll be back in a minute" for I was anxious to get my "wheels" back on the road. I got up and went out the door of the roadhouse and into the mechanic's workshop. I hadn't been there more than two minutes when I heard a commotion. I looked through the glass and saw my new acquaintance being forcefully led away by three tall men in suits. One had a hand over his mouth and all three had him solidly in their grip and were dragging him out the door. I ran in but by the time I got to them they had bound and gagged him and he was lying in the back seat of an enormous black car.

Now, I want to tell you about this car. I have never seen a car like it – it was long, wide and sleek and streamlined, as if it could fly as well as move on the road. If you had told me it was capable of flight, I would have believed you. If you had told me it could drive off a bank and scoot across water I would have believed you. If you had told me it could travel under water, I would have believed you. It just exuded by its appearance the impression of being engineered to have capabilities beyond the reach of human imagination. And it was bigger than normal cars as if it was designed to accommodate giants. And it gleamed in such an immaculate black I had never seen before. It was deep black, yet iridescent at the same time in a way I cannot describe to you. The men in suits were also immaculate – yet though they were in suits they were also immensely tall and muscular, none of them was under six and a half feet, I think they were all nearer seven feet, but their suits fitted them like they had been tailored. Their suits also somehow looked as if they were designed, not just to make them look slick, but to enable them to indulge in extreme physical activity, like dragging my new acquaintance to the car. They had also glowing, healthy, shining skin as if they lived off the fat of the land and had found the ability to avoid all the pestilences, diseases and afflictions that age normal people.

"Thank you for holding him for us" one said, smiling, coming over to me. "You've done the world a service. He's a very dangerous man."

I then noticed he had in his hand a sealable plastic bag such as is used in hospitals for disposing of waste, and in it were the gun and knife the fellow had had under his coat, so obviously they had been no use to him in the way of avoiding capture.

"These will be taken for forensic examination. We've been after him for some time, now we've nabbed him".

I have no idea why they assumed I had been "holding him". I raised my hands as if to say "Hold him? All I did was talk to him for a while".

"What did he say to you?" said the second man, smiling, but with hint of inerrogatory suspicion.

I was defensive, I didn't want to be bound and gagged and thrown into the car also. I affected ignorance.

"Oh, nothing, really. He just …blathered about various things.. I didn't really follow what he was saying… he made no sense…..I was slightly afraid of him." I had a cowardly impulse to ingratiate myself to these fear-inspiring, giant-size, streamlined men in suits.

"He's a very dangerous fellow" repeated the first man. "You've done the world a great service. He spreads dangerous ideas and false rumours that could create great instability, and great distrust in authority. We could have nabbed him before, but we felt it would cause more trouble to have him removed than to leave him to roam free. We thought if we removed him it would only give him credibility. We thought no-one was believing this ridiculous ideas. But we discovered people were beginning to believe him. The time had come for him to be removed. He was a slippery fellow, and cunning, or we would have nabbed him before. Thank you for holding him."

Then, he shook my hand in thanks. I have never hand my hand squeezed with such a demoniacally strong grip. It was as if the fellow was possessed of such strength he couldn't control it. Occasionally, still, I bend my fingers a certain way and feel a stab of pain as if somewhere in my bone structure I have sustained irreparable damage.

My former interlocutor, "the man on the run", was lying now on the back seat bound and gagged, but writhing, squirming and staring at me with a wild look. He could not speak, but his face told me what words could not. It was saying "Help me, help me, or if you cannot, please tell others what I have told you.. it may be too late.. but you must try..you must try...you must try..."

I shall never forget the look on that face till I die.

WAITING FOR ANNA

Ron was a 55 year old deserted husband whose wife had got everything including the house and most of his assets. He was condemned to living in a pokey flat and scraping by on his pension since he could no longer get work.

But there was one person who was the light of his life – his 28 year old youngest daughter, Anna. He had two daughters, and the older always sided with her mother, and wouldn't speak to him, leave alone visit him, while the youngest, Anna had always taken his side. The strange thing was she was the opposite of him in some ways – political outlook, temperament and looks, while the elder one, who now wouldn't even talk to him, was like her father in all those things.

Anna had a highly paid executive job that occupied her time what seemed like 25 hours a day and eight days a week. She was always winging off overseas where she was desperately needed to troubleshoot for or take control of some distant office of the organization for which she worked. In fact she was now more often away than at home. But whenever she was in town she always made time to see her father at least once. There had evolved a tradition that she would come over to his place (he would look out the window to see the Porsche pull up outside and park in his dingy street) and he would cook dinner for her.

They could have gone out somewhere, but it was more intimate to have dinner under his roof, and it was an expression that he could do something for himself totally without the assistance of his wife.

He was so proud when people used to remark "Who was that piece I saw walking up to your door yesterday? She looked like a movie star. Real estate agent or something was it?"

"That's my daughter!" he would say. "Isn't she great! She's not in real estate, but she could buy and sell this whole street ten times over if she wanted". And the person would often look him up and down, at his balding scrawny, weather-beaten form and say, jokingly, with disbelief "How could an old so-and-so like you produce something like that?" which only made him swell his shoulders even more proudly and say "Wonderful, isn't it? Isn't she just great?"

Whenever she was coming he would spend two days cleaning the place, at least, all the parts of it that she was going to see. It wasn't that he was particularly dirty or untidy, but it was a daggy flat to start with and was hard to keep clean, and he wanted it to be absolutely spotless. It couldn't be too good for Anna. He would clean the rubbish off the footpath where she was going to park, he would get rid of the discarded mattresses and all the other trash tenants had left on the landings that she would have to pass between getting out of the car and arriving at his door. Unfortunately he couldn't do anything about the unpleasant cooking smells that often wafted along the landings from the other flats. He would hire a lawnmower and trim the tiny patch of grass that the block of flats possessed. He would paint over any graffiti that would be within her range of vision when she walked in. It might be back in a few days but at least he could stop her seeing it. He always felt, not only that he didn't want her to see these objectionable things, but that he was "putting out a red carpet" for her when he made these preparations.

Whenever she arrived for one of these visits it had become a tradition she would bring him a new necktie from one of the exotic places she had visited since she saw him last, with some distinctive pattern or logo on it to mark its place of origin. Not that he wanted all those ties to wear, of course - most of them were so garish or had patterns so bizarre you wouldn't even want to wear them - it was just a tradition, and he had them all hung in a row on his living room wall. There was one from the Dubai Cricket Club He thought he knew where Dubai was but he didn't know they'd ever played cricket there. There was one from The Edinburgh Institute of the Finance Industry, and one from the Washington Diplomats' Club, and one from Brazil, and one with Japanese gobbledey-gook on it from some client in Tokyo – it went on and on. He wouldn't wear one in a fit, but whenever he saw them he'd think –wow! – what a daughter I've got that she's been to all those places!

Actually their gaudy patterns arranged in a row livened up the place. It was just a little in joke between them. And when she first arrived she would always, after accepting a glass of her favourite wine from him, plonk herself down in an armchair, kick her shoes off, and just talk, and talk, and talk, as if it was an opportunity to let all the accumulated worries and frustrations of her job come out. It always turned out she did most of the talking, he just sat there enthralled by everything that came out of her mouth, it all seemed so important, and momentous, and glamourous. He didn't have a clue what she actually did from day to day, it was all a lot of gobbledygook of rates and loans and derivatives and hedge funds and smedge funds and other financial gibberish that was beyond him, but he knew it was very important otherwise they wouldn't be paying her so much money to do it and her time wouldn't be in such high demand.

It was like the clothes she wore. She wasn't exactly built like a fashion model, she was a bit out of condition, a bit large around the hips and slightly round shouldered due to the long hours she spent at a sedentary job, as a result of which she used to always wear long skirts to hide her odd-shaped legs, and loose-fitting outfits to hide her unshapely hips, but he could tell the clothes she wore, (and though she didn't have to dress up when she came to visit him but she always did) were expensive, exclusively tailored and stylish according to the latest fashions, if only because sometimes he thought that because they looked so bad (to him) that they must be good!

He liked it also when she talked about all the office politics and the gossip and the indiosyncrasies of the people she worked with. They were high falutin' business men and executives and their secretaries, but they were still human beings with all the eccentricities and strange ways and faults that normal people have. He could tell it was a treat for her to be able to speak her mind about the people she worked with in a way she wasn't able to when she was with them.

That evening he had the table all prepared with an immaculate white table cloth, (he actually went out and bought a new one every time she came just to make sure it was spotless) painstakingly polished china and cutlery, and even a vase of real flowers placed right in the middle. (He was always felt a bit self conscious going out and buying flowers and bringing them home, but he never missed doing it). Instead of that dingy flat, when the table was all set, if you lowered the lights, and didn't look too hard for cracks in the walls, you could have been in a fancy restaurant. And he would dress specially for her, in "smart casual".

He always got in a special kind of wine she liked, (which wasn't cheap!) and just for that evening he would grit his teeth and steel himself to actually drink it himself, to please her, pretending he liked it. He wouldn't have touched it with a barge pole ordinarily, because he didn't like wine, he was a beer drinker, or when he really wanted to get blotto – port. but in a way it was good, because it meant he would only drink one glass of it, and sip it gradually. whereas if he drank beer all evening he would have got drunk, and he didn't want her to see him drunk.

She had seen him that way too much in her early years.

He always timed the cooking so it would be almost ready just when she arrived. Tonight it was roast chicken, potatoes and three vegetables, preceeded by pea and ham soup which he made himself, and succeeded by luscious cherry pie and cream which he also made himself. He had become quite a good cook since the break up of his marriage. He had learnt by trial and error, using simple ingredients and basic, traditional ways of preparation. He didn't want to buy in prepared stuff, it wouldn't have been good enough, and nothing was too good for Anna.

She was due to arrive at 7 o'clock. She was never strictly on time, but he expected that, because he knew she was always busy right up to the time she left and she would be coming straight from work. Then at 6.30 the first call came.

It was Anna.

"Look I'm really sorry Dad, I'll be a bit late, I've got this job I've just got to finish tonight, and it's taking me longer than I thought, I'll probably be only another half an hour, I'm really, really sorry".

Another half an hour, he thought. It took her three quarters of an hour to get to his place, that meant she wouldn't be there until a quarter to eight.

But he put on his most blasé and chivalrous tome.

"Oh, that's all right. I'll just be glad to see you when you do get here. You know that".

After he hung up the phone, he figured he would turn the stove off, and restart it in about half an hour.

There was suddenly a knock at the door. For a stupid moment he thought it might be Anna, but then, how could it be, if she was still at work, and anyway she would have buzzed the buzzer on the security board if it was her, and even if someone had let her in because they were going out at the same time and recognized her, she would have called out in excitement when she knocked.

He opened the door. It was the annoying woman in the next flat. She was misshapen, unprepossessing, in her 60s and smelt, not only of herself, but of cats, which she kept in abundance, and of alcohol and stale tobacco smoke. She would pester him sometimes several times in one day about anything, and talk to him familiarly as if they were old buddies.

"The ongoing story of my water heater...." she started, as if that was a subject which he had been waiting with bated breath to hear the next instalment of. He couldn't just tell her to go away, because she was such a pathetic old thing, but he tried to look as irritated and pre-occupied and impatient as possible, without saying outright that he was.

"After all that money I spent having it fixed myself and getting the landlord to pay me now he says it needs a new heater and I shouldn't have paid to get the old one fixed!"

She suddenly looked him up and down seeing he was so neatly attired.

"Well, aren't you dressed up to the nines!"

She then peered round him with her parrot-like eyes and saw the table laid with the nice white table-cloth, flowers, and neatly laid out crockery and cutlery for two people.

"Oooh, you must have a lady-friend coming!" she cooed.

He couldn't say to her "mind your own business", but he could scowl.

"My daughter's coming for dinner" he said with as much of an unpleasant tone in it as he could manage, as if to say "Why don't you mind your own business you repulsive old hen and anyway that obviously means I'm busy preparing for her".

"Oooh! The one who comes here sometimes, I've seen her on the stairs, isn't she beautiful, and elegant – those expensive clothes she wears. You must be so lucky to have a daughter like that. She must have a good job to be able to afford such expensive clothes. And is that her fancy car I see parked outside sometimes?"

(Nothing that happened within half a mile of the block of flats where they lived escaped her notice).

"Oooh, she must have a good job. That's like my nephew, he's got this fancy job and earns all these big piles of money my family never heard of. She must be so smart. I don't know where these kids got their brains, do you? Not from us, eh!"

He thought "Speak for yourself!"

She peered round him at the set table again and then beamed into his eyes.

"You'll have to have me for dinner one day and I'll tell you my whole life story!"

He thought "You'd be lucky!" It was about the two hundred and fifty thousandth time she'd suggested that. He reflected he'd probably heard her whole life story about ten times over anyway, and was none the better for knowing it.

"Anyway I can see you're busy I'll let you go now!"

She made a faint sideways movement away from his doorway to give credibility to her words. The trouble was, that statement "I'll let you go now" was usually a false promise, followed by another five minutes of yabbering.

However this time he was just plain brusque with her and said "Yes, thanks, that's fine, I'm sorry to hear about your water heater, see you later" and shut the door, not exactly in her face, but almost.

He turned away from the door and reflected having her darken his doorway when he was expecting Anna was like hoping to win the lottery and getting a parking ticket instead.

He took the lid of the saucepan and started poking the vegetables to see just how far they were cooked, then he looked in the oven to see if maybe he should turn it on again now anyway. Then there was another knock on the door,

He opened it ready to really blow his top if it was that awful woman again. But it someone equally un-wanted, a little runt who also lived in the building and was perpetually "borrowing" money.

He looked at Ron with his head on one side and the usual ambiguous smile and shifty eyes.

"You couldn't see your way to lending me five dollars, could you? I'll pay you back tomorrow, for sure" he said slowly.

Ron, looking at him in a knowing way, simply took five dollars from his pocket and gave it to him. He knew he would never see it again. But if he said "no" he might get a window mysteriously broken, or his car scratched, or some rubbish dropped on his step, or something nasty put in his letterbox. Paying off this creep was a sort of insurance policy, or more exactly a protection racket, that cost him on the aver-age five or ten dollars a week. The little runt probably did the same thing to everyone in the building, and made enough to live on or finance his drug habit that way, who knows? Sometimes he would disap-pear for weeks or months, but he always came back again. Ron assumed at those times be was in gaol, but who knew? It was a waste of time complaining to the police about any damage the creep inflicted on his property. They'd say "Have you got any witnesses, sir?" Unlike the awful woman the little runt didn't peer around and look inside the room he just said with the same grin "I'll pay you back tomorrow, for sure" and turned and walked away.

Ron reflected as he closed the door, well, at least he was one pest who wouldn't be back that evening, because he never came more than once in the same day.

He thought, as he always did, having Anna appear in a place like this, was like a beautiful flower suddenly sprouting out of a compost heap.

Not that she was ever fazed by the malodorous and dingy area where he lived - the scruffy people, the broken fences, the rubbish in the streets, the dilapidated houses, the cracked windows, the screaming of families having vociferous arguments, the drying clothes on balconies, the broken toys in front yards, the unkempt lawns, the abandoned cars in the street..... She never even as much as remarked on these things, but just was careful where she put her dainty feet, or picked up her skirts a bit to stop them getting dirty, if necessary, as if any place where her father was, was a place worth coming to, no matter what. He knew she would come to visit him anywhere – if he was on an island in the middle of a swamp, a broken down shack in the desert, or a mansion on a hill, it would have made no difference to her, but he wished he had better surroundings to show her.

She was the light of his life, he wouldn't have known any point in going on living it wasn't for her – it was the one thing that made up for his poverty, the wreck of his marriage, the loss of his ability to earn a living, for his dingy accommodation, and the repulsive people who cohabited his building. Her existence made him feel that part of him, no matter what else was a wreck, was good, because she was his flesh and blood.

She had actually offered to buy him a place of residence once, which she could have afforded to do, but he had said "No", he should be looking after her, she was his daughter, not she looking after him. He would have spent his last cent on her if he had to, but of course she didn't need him to, and he would have done anything for her. But because she had everything, there was nothing he could do for her. However, he had let her pay for major work on his teeth, to give him a virtually perfect mouth, as a present for his 53rd birthday. It was way more than he could ever have afforded himself. In a way he felt rather humiliated about letting her spend so much money on him, but then he justified it by thinking, at least she wouldn't have to look at a mouth full of broken teeth when she came to visit him!

Once he had driven her to the airport and although he had made great efforts to see everything in his dilapidated car was spotless, she had torn her skirt on a piece of wire sticking out of the upholstery that he hadn't noticed, and got a spot of grease on it as well. He had almost cried and said I'll pay to have it dry cleaned, I'll pay so you can buy a new skirt..." but she had just dismissed it with a "Don't worry, Dad.It's nothing" and it had gone straight out of her mind.

Now he couldn't even afford to own a car.

So different to her mother. If her mother had torn her dress in his car or got a smidgin of grease on her from it she would have made out like it was the end of the world. "You can buy me another one for that. I'll never get that repaired, That stain won't come out. You can't get these anymore. You're so inconsiderate...." He could imagine almost word for word what she'd say.

Anything he ever did wrong was World War Three and a calamity. Anything she did wrong was his fault. "There you are you've made me drop that dish... there you are you made me forget my keys ...there you are you've given me a headache, I won't sleep now, I'll be late for work in the morning..."

She knew the things that irritated him and she went out of her way to say them. He'd come home from work with a sour look on his face, and as soon as he walked in the door she'd look at him and say "Are you in one of your funny moods this evening?"

Was there anything more calculated to put someone in a "funny mood" that to have it said to them

"Are you in one of your 'funny moods?' whether they were or not?

Or she would say, if she could see he didn't want to talk about his day

"So was went wrong at work today?"

If he just grunted and shrugged, as a way or saying he didn't want to talk about it, she would sit back, fold her arms, stare at him provocatively and prod him verbally. "No, come on. What went wrong at work today? Why are you in such a bad mood?"

Then he sometimes would make the mistake of actually telling her.

For instance he might say "It's this new guy, Smith.....who just started there...I have to work with him all day....I can't stand him I JUST CAN'T STAND HIM!". And he would thump the table.

Instead of just accepting his words, she had to then say, while getting up and turning her back on him "He's probably a very nice man. You should just get to know him better. You're hard to get on with, that's all! It 's probably all your fault".

And of course then it would be on for young and old.

He would jump to his feet and start barking at her. "How would you know he's a nice person? You've never even met him! How would you know if he was nice? That's your trouble – you're always passing opinions about people you've never even met!".

"Oh, you're Mr Bad-Tempered this evening are you? Don't bother to come home if you're in a bad mood, we can do without you!"

"Don't bother to come home? To my house? Oh, that' s fine, I can't come home to my house, which I've paid for! Listen, missus...."

And so on.

And yes, he did have a drinking problem. And yes, he had hit her a couple of times. But she went out of her way to push him to that point, so she could be the victim. But because of these things, he didn' t have a leg to stand on when it came to the divorce.

In a way he thought it would have been good if Anna was married and started a family, he would have grandchildren to boast about, and what grandchildren they would be, with her as a mother! But in another way he was secretly glad that she hadn't, though he was ashamed of himself for thinking that. The truth was, for a start, he couldn't visualise any man being good enough for her. She made casual reference sometimes to some man-friend she was seeing, but she never went into detail (not that he wanted to know detail!) and he was always left with the impression she wasn't that fussed about men and was so totally absorbed in her job it didn't leave much time for that side of life, even though she must be meeting a ton of eligibles every day. In a way, selfish also as it was, he was even glad she wasn't exactly a ravishing beauty, not nearly as attractive even as he mother had been when she was that age, because if she had been, maybe she would have not have been so devoted to her career and would have had all sorts of men chasing her. Though he knew it was selfish of him he often thought if she had appeared on his doorstep with a husband, or a serious boyfriend, it would have jarred, he would immediately have seen him as a competitor for her attention. And what was worse, with all her globetrotting, supposing, horror of horrors, she was to marry someone from another country and stay in that country!

The phone rang again. Maybe that was Anna!

"Do you know who I saw coming out of number 2?....."

No such luck, It was next door again! And it really annoyed him, if he needed anything more to annoy him, the way she didn't even bother to announce herself but just assumed he would recognise her voice.

"Who?" he asked bluntly, making sure he sounded as short as possible.

"Her ex. I think they're back together again! After all he did to her! Isn't that something?"

"Yes. That's very interesting" he said is as uninterested and blunt a tone as he could muster.

What did she expect? That he was going to have a long conversation about the ins and outs of the ongoing domestic saga at number 2?

There was short silence, and he knew she was debating whether she had any grounds to keep him on the phone any longer.

"Oh, well, I'll let you go, now. I suppose your beautiful daughter's there, is she?"

That made him boil with anger.

"No, she's not" he shouted, and kicked himself straightaway, because he didn't want her to know how much it was upsetting him.

"Ooh, I wonder why she's late. Perhaps she's not coming.."

"I've got to go now" he said peremptorily and hung up. He would have taken the phone off the hook if he wasn't waiting on a call from Anna.

Then the phone rang straightaway again. He was convinced it was the awful woman again, and he actually opened his mouth to scream abuse at her, and an angry "Uh!" just slipped out, before he heard Anna'a voice.

"Dad, I'm really sorry, I'm going to be held up even more, I've just had a phone call from the States, I've got to re-do everything. I'm so sorry… It'll take me a while.. but I will get there, I will, no matter what…I've just got to finish this…it's a major crisis over there."

He managed his most diplomatic and understanding tone.

"Oh, that's alright. I'll still be here. You just finish… whatever you've got to do…That' all right."

"I'm really sorry, Dad. I really am. I just had no idea this was going to happen. If anything I thought I'd be early tonight, but all this has happened. I'm really sorry, Dad".

"You just do what you have to so, I'll still be here"

There was a short silence, and he knew she was desperately trying to find words worth saying to express her apology even further, but she couldn't.

"Bye, Dad"

She hung up the phone.

Even in his own rage, he knew how she was feeling, When you really want to apologise for something, but can't find the right words, or enough words to do it. But that didn't ease his mounting rage.

He started walking round the flat like a caged lion as was his way, punching one fist into his other hand. He could have watched TV, listened to the radio, read a newspaper, read a book, but he was too pre-occupied to do anything but inwardly fume over the situation.

She had never in all the years actually missed one of their dinner appointments. Sometimes the time between them was three weeks, sometimes two months, once he had gone 10 months without seeing her, but she had never not actually made it when they had made a time. Once she had not arrived until 10pm and it had been so late when it came time to go she had slept on the couch over night, but she had never not actually made it. That was one thing that buoyed him up now.

Then he started breaking his circuits of the room to go neurotically to the window and look out through the venetian blinds to see if her car was out there, which of course it wasn't.

He had found it hard to "meet someone" since the demise of his marriage, even though unattached men in his age group were supposed to be in demand.

He wasn't exactly Clark Gable, though on the plus side he wasn't overweight, but he was balding, and though he was skinny he could never get rid of a bit of a paunch. He had tried all sorts of diets and exercises but it would never go away. And when he met anyone for the first time, and they were talking, the conversation always came back to why his wife had left him. He could see the look in their eyes, and tell by their probing questions, that the implication in their minds was "If his wife left him what' s wrong with him? If she didn't want him, why should I want him?" If he had been a good liar, he could have made up some story about her being unfaithful to him, or being bad mother, or a crazy, or something, but he wasn't a good liar, and he was not dishonest like that by nature anyway. Furthermore, he figured if he had told some lies, the other woman would have seen through them.

He reflected often with bitterness at the way of the world, that If he had been a serial philanderer with a string of divorces and dumped girlfriends and broken hearts behind him, they would have liked him better! They would think "Well, if all those women liked him, he must have something going for him….."

And whenever they saw the place where he lived, unless it was as bad or better than where they lived, that put them off as well. Of course, if they lived in a place that was as bad as or worse than his, well, he wouldn't want them!

And after he could no longer afford to run a car, that put him out of reach of female companions even further.

He looked back over a concatenation of depressing encounters from meetings in clubs, blind dates, friends of friends, even dating services, each one ending, it seemed to him when he looked back, with him coming home alone and miserable and let down to his empty, dingy home, in the squalid building, the only bright star there being those photos of Anna that greeted him, and reassured him he was still a human being of value and not a piece of refuse no longer needed by society.

Because of his baldness and his weatherbeaten face he looked older than he was. One of the most embarrassing things that had ever happened to him was an occasion when he had been out with a woman who he knew was older than him, and when the conversation had got round to a discussion to how the difference in their ages might affect the chance of any future relationship, he had said in his blunt way "I don't mind you being older than me" and she had responded with a most peculiar uncomprehending look that dumbfounded him, until he realised it was because she had thought from his appearance he was older than her.

And when in the course of an evening's conversation he got round to waxing lyrical about his daughter Anna, and how proud he was of her, which he nearly always did, because it was about the only thing in his life he could dredge up to make conversation about that he was proud of, he could see in their eyes they were mentally comparing his appearance with the image he was painting of Anna, and half the time thinking he was making it all up.

What a joke life was! He had done the right thing, made a marriage and a home and raised two children, he had gone without to make them into something, and, apart from having the devotion of his daughter, had ended up with nothing! If he had stayed single he would have been sitting pretty!

Just then he heard a great bumping and scraping and some cursing from out in the corridor. He opened his front door, thinking "What the heck is that?"

Two scruffy young men who he knew also lived in the block were endeavouring to shift an enormous and very cheap and ugly table down the hallway. It was almost as wide as the hall, and obviously very heavy.

"Found this in the street, and we lobbed it up here, now we found it's too big for our room, so we're taking it out again" explained one.

"Could you give us a hand?" the other one said, looking at Ron with a helpless stare as if he was about to give up on the whole thing.

"Maybe we could leave it here" the first one suggested "Someone else might want it".

Dumping a table in the middle of a hallway because they couldn't be bothered shifting it any further is just the sort of thing the kind of people who lived in the block would do.

Ron exploded.

"My daughter's coming here this evening. She doesn't what to see this great piece of junk stuck in the hallway blocking her way. She'll hardly be able to get past!".

The first one looked at him as if he had just had an ingenious idea as to how to blackmail Ron into helping them.

"Well, you better help us get it downstairs then" he said with a meaningful look, that suggested "or else we will dump it here".

Ron set to to give them a hand to get it down the hallway, and then onto the first flight of stairs, It was a matter of turning it on its side and gradually manoeuvring it round. With a lot of cursing and shouting "lift it up lift up! No, not that far. Turn it round, turn it round. Tilt it over this way, this way not that way" they somehow got it half way. Just then Ron's phone rang again and he rushed back to his flat, leaving the two straining on their muscles to keep the table in the position where it was until he got back. He was sure it was Anna.

But it was the woman next door again "What's all that bumping a and scraping I hear in the hallway?"

Of course, she could have come out to see for herself, but she had to use the telephone, didn't she?

"I'm just helping two idiots move a table" he said angrily.

"What table? Who are they? Where are you moving it to?"

He was so incensed at having to be doing the ridiculous thing he was doing and at it not being Anna, he just hung up on her, and went back to the stairs.

Somehow, after some minutes of bruised knuckles and sweat, they got it down, and out the front door. The two scruffbags were all for dumping it right at the front gate, but he insisted they help him take it round the corner where it would be out of the sight of Anna when she came. Carrying it in the open on the flat footpath wasn't much of a task, anyway, He wasn't one for dumping rubbish in front of other peoples' property, but today he just wanted to get the filthy great thing out of sight to minimise the visual pollution Anna had to suffer when she came.

Just after he got back inside his flat the security buzzer went off.

Was it Anna?

He pressed it.

"Is that the Camilleri's?" came a strange voice.

His heart sank. "No there's no −one by that name here".

Are you sure?"

('No, I don't know my own name, I'd better go and check! There might be a whole family I don't know about hiding in my flat' he thought of saying.)

"I said 'no', there's no-one by that name here!"

"This is the address I've got for them".

"Well, you've got the wrong address!"

Then in another minute it buzzed again.

"Do you know if the Camilleris are in this building?"

"No!" he answered brusquely, "I don't know the name of everyone in the building! I've never heard of them!"

"Were they in you place there before you? How long have you been there?"

"Too long! Look, I can't help you. Don't buzz me again!":.

But they did.

"Do you know if there's any Camillieris in this street?'

They weren't even apologetic about wasting his time.

"No! I've never heard of them. I wouldn't know if they're in this street or not! Do you think I know everyone in the street? Don't buzz me again!"

If he had been working, he could have afforded a better place., but after his marriage broke up, he had been sacked, because he turned up late so much, after getting drunk the night before to drown his sorrows, and the final straw had been when he had blown up in the face of the foreman and abused him.

After some time of unemployment, he had finally got back into his trade and he got 18 months out of it, but he was retrenched through no fault of his own, the company was losing money and closed down. It was after that he had a really long stretch of unemployment.

He suddenly found the people interviewing him were 20 or 30 years younger than him. He knew what they were thinking, They were thinking, "This guy's 55, I'm 22. If I give him the job he'll be a 55 year old with a 22 year old boss. What does that prove? It proves that he's a total failure in life! And, boy, will I let him know it!" And he didn't brush up well at interviews. His voice was naturally harsh and abrasive, he was balding, and scrawny, and pale-faced, he wasn't physically pre-possessing. If only he could have lit up a fag at interviews, he would have relaxed a bit and performed better. Whenever he was at an interview, he just felt like a loser, and felt he was appearing to look like a loser.

He now needed glasses to read small print close up, and once at the last interview he had been to before he gave up looking they had handed him an operating manual and said 'See if you can make sense of that. If you can't – you're no good for this job!" He had had to get his reading glasses out and put them on because the print was so small, and as he did so he had seen out of the corner of his eye one of the two interviewers smirking at the other with a look that said "This guy's past it. He's no use to us He has to use reading glasses to look at the manual". It was so humiliating!

It was for all these reasons he had found it hard to get jobs. And when he did get a job, he just couldn't take being ordered around by someone half his age. Somehow, he also found, he just wasn't fast enough as he should have been and he couldn't pick up new processes and adjust to new machines, and like the punks who interviewed him, these young johnny-come-latelies he worked with really made him know it. The only thing that kept him sane in this period was the thought of his daughter Anna and what a giant of self-achievement she was. He would listen around the lunch table to men near his age talking about their kids, and, many of them having turned out ne'er do wells and misfits, (like their parents actually, he thought) and he would be secretly laughing at them inside. Their kids and Anna didn't even belong in the same universe.

He had photos of Anna at all stages of her life all over his flat, big ones on the wall, smaller ones in little frames on pieces of furniture. He had photos of her graduation, of her speaking at seminars, of her accepting merit and achievement awards from her company at grand, glittering, corporate gatherings, photos of her at well known landmarks in exotic locations all over the world taken in those rare moments when she had time for sight-seeing while overseas, and in every photo, she didn't look like a bathing beauty, but she looked so well groomed, so self-assured, so sophisticated, so focussed, so successful, so much like an achiever, so much like a person in command of their destiny. The opposite of him, he often reflected. But his one great achievement was that he had produced and brought up this wonderful daughter.

Once he had gone into her office when they were going out for lunch together, and when he had been sitting in the in the fantastically sumptuous reception area, people coming past had thought he was a courier, or a messenger, they couldn't have imagined he was related to one of their executives. When she had come out for him finally, while he was ready to just walk out the door with her, she had taken him into the main part of the enormous office and introduced him to all her colleagues and subordinates with a proud "I want you to meet my Dad!" He could tell by the way they spoke to her, and the looks they gave her, and the way they stood up as soon as she walked into their offices, that she was a person of great stature and importance in the company, but not only that, a person who was respected, and not only that, liked, and liked, not only by the other executives, but her underlings as well. Most of them said, as they shook his hand "You must be very proud of your daughter!". Some had even said "This place would fall apart without her!" and they looked at him as if he must have some magic within him to have produced such an offspring. The fact that they were all well groomed and in suits, while he was so obviously working class and in cheap clothes, with gnarled hands and a weather beaten face from years of working in the sun, fazed her not at all. Now, how many daughters in her position would have done that?

If he had had to go to his wife's place of work to meet her, she would have told him to wait for her in the street, or in the car park, as if he was a smelly dog.

When he looked back on his life he found, to his surprise, the times he remembered he had most enjoyed were when he was with his kids, his two daughters. When they were very young, five and seven years old, he remembered often sitting with his wife at the beach, or in a park watching the two playing together, throwing sand at each other, or chasing each other, and just having fun and enjoying themselves, and though even at that stage he and his wife were at loggerheads, he used to like sitting with her watching their two little daughters just having fun. And later, when the estrangement had become even wider Anna, who was a bit of a "tomboy" had liked to go to with him to the football while his wife and his other daughter had done whatever they wanted to do, and Anna had yelled and screamed and cheered and jumped up and down in their team's coloured scarfs, and booed alongside him, with the best. In fact, she had been usually more vociferous than he was! Sometimes he had been scared she was going to run out on the field and bop the referee one on the nose! He remembered those cold, shivering evenings they had spent together, standing under an umbrella in the rain, eating cheap hot dogs and drinking bad coffee out of paper cups, their eyes riveted on the game to the last whistle, and going home unbelievably elated or downtrodden according to whether their team had won or lost, It had seemed so physically uncomfortable at the time, if enjoyable, but now he remembered those times with only fondness. She had kept fanatically exact records of the statistics of their team, the number of tackles in each match, the try-scorers, the goal scorers, the penalties for and against, she was a walking encyclopaedia of the sport. He remembered thinking then that her steel-trap of a mind and her obsessive attention to detail indicated potential for a good career in some field where it would be an asset in later life. And she liked to go fishing with him as well. He couldn't remember either of them ever catching much, but when he looked back on those long hours they had spent on the windy pier waiting for that elusive tug on the line, and coming home with sand in their shoes and sunburnt and smelling of salt and seaweed and fish, he remembered those times with fondness as well.

Suddenly the phone rang. Anna? he thought.

"Who's these Camellieris those people were asking for? Do you know any Cammileris? I know everyone in the building and I don't know any Camillieris. there's ino one by that name here! Do you know who they are? What are they buzzing us all for when there's no-one by that name here...?"

Who else would it be? It was Next Door.

He would have really blown his top at her but he didn't want to be in a state of anger when

Anna arrived, however he made sure his voice was a blunt and off-putting as possible. "No I don't know who they are. It was the wrong address. It's probably way up the other end of the street. It's probably the wrong suburb. Look, I'm waiting for a call from my daughter. Please don't disturb me again!"

"OK, I won't disturb you again". The hurt feeling her voice was palpable. She thought she had the right to ring him any hour of the day or night and engage him in conversation and get his fullest attention.

What a place Anna was forced to come to just to see her Dad, he thought. People you didn't know buzzing you all night looking for other people you didn't know – desperates shifting worthless pieces of furniture around the hallway – loonies from next door pestering you on the phone all day, thieves "borrowing" money from you – not to mention the smells of cheap cooking and occasional unpleasant raucous raised voices emanating from the other flats.

The length of the stays she spent overseas seemed to increase all the time, The first time she had gone it had been two weeks, the next three weeks, the next two months, the next six months, the next almost a year. It was understandable, in a way, because her position in the company was becoming more and more important and she was becoming more and more indispensable. By a simple process of extrapolation, he was dreading that one day she would have to stay there permanently and not come back!

The phone rang again. Somehow he knew it was Next Door.

He snatched up the phone in a fit of anger and screamed "Will you go away!".

"Dad!"

It was Anna.

He was brought up with a start, and mentally kicked himself at the thought he might have hurt her feelings. "Oh, love, I didn't know it was you, love, I'm sorry! I thought it was that awful woman next door I told you about who pesters me day and night about nothing. "Then suddenly he really perked up. "Are you on your way?"

There was an apologetic and almost nervous tone in her voice. "That's what I was ringing for, Dad. I've....I've been held up some more. I'm ....I'm just waiting for this call from the States. As soon as it comes I can leave. But I have to wait for it....."

There was a pause as if she was debating what next to say, and couldn't find words.

"It shouldn't be too long...."

It sounded so much like those telephone operators, when you are ringing up a company, who come one the line at intervals and say mechanically "Shouldn't be too much longer..." and then keep you waiting another ten minutes.

"Oh, that's alright..it's just that..I've got everything ready.. you know..and it's getting late...."

He was just starting to show traces of impatience, and he didn't want to.

"OK, Dad..." Then she hung up with a very soft "Bye" He knew it wasn't abruptness, he knew it was just there weren't words she could find to apologise with.

For some reason he suddenly started thinking about the time he had cooked dinner for his wife. It had been a kind of reconciliation attempt. He had gone out of his way to do everything just right and surprise her, and she had just sat at the table with a bored, supercilious look on her face, watching everything he did, just waiting for him to do something she could find fault with. He remembered how he had placed a big vase of flowers in the middle of the table and hoped she would be pleased. "There, lovely flowers!" he had said. She had touched one of the stems vaguely, turned up one side of her lip and said "I think that's the kind I'm allergic to".

Then when the whole table was laid, he had placed some bread and butter with it.

Out of everything that was on the table, she picked on the bread and butter.

"What have you got bread and butter on the table for?"

"I just thought someone might want it, like they have in restaurants, you know how they give you garlic bread, but I haven't got any garlic bread."

She made a look as if to say "How ignorant you are" and said "It's just that you don't normally put bread and butter on a table with a cooked dinner, that's all".

He could have blown his top then, but he didn't.

Then she started eating, picking at the food gingerly as if it was contaminated.

"Why have you cooked the vegetables so much?"

He wanted to say "Because you never cook then enough!" but just shrugged and grinned and tried to look as if he was really enjoying his, anyway.

"You know I don't like parsnips. Why did you put them in?"

He suddenly remembered, she had once said she didn't like parsnips. But so what? It wasn't the end of the world!

"You haven't cooked the meat enough!"

Of course, everything would be not cooked enough or cooked too much wouldn't it?

She nibbled very slowly a bit more of what was on her plate with a bored look on her face and then suddenly pushed it away with a sneer and got up.

"Actually I'm not hungry tonight. Give it to the dog!"

Then she called out the name of her oldest daughter.

"Do you want to go down the Italian place? I just feel like some pasta! I can't eat this sludge your father's cooked up!"

When he had first met her, he had been infatuated with her. For a short time, he had thought nothing could be more beautiful than her face. Now, when he saw a photo of that face, and what was behind it, all he thought was "bitch!"

Just then there was a knock on the door.

Could it be Anna? Could she have been just playng a little joke on him, ringing from somewhere just round the corner to say she would be late, then arriving a few minutes later and surprising him? Someone could have let her in the front door!

But he could tell it was not the way she would knock anyway.

It was two little urchins who he knew lived in a another part of the building. One had a ridiculous-looking small dog in his arms.

"Mister is this your dog? We found it wandering in the garden. It looks like its leg's broken"

It was one of those ugly creatures that have no hair, big pointed ears, and eyes too big for their head, and you know are good for nothing but yapping and getting under your feet.

"No, it's not mine" he said impatiently.

"Does you know who owns it"

"No I don't know"

For a second he thought of telling them to knock on the door of the awful woman in the next flat and tell them "It'd just go well with all her cats! She'd love it" but thought better of it.

"Someone must own it!"

He looked at it and thought he would be very surprised if anyone wanted to own it.

"Well, no-one owns it here!"

The kid looked at the pooch he had in his arms forlornly.

"Can we leave it with you, mister? Our mum won't have dogs in the flat"

He didn't blame her.

"NO!"

And he slammed the door.

He had been pacing the floor before, now the interruption had made him feel like doing something else. He just sat down in an armchair, gripped the arms, and tried to collect himself. He felt like having something to drink, but he never did before Anna came. He didn't want to greet her with the smell of alcohol on his breath. He tried breathing deeply and slowly, telling himself that nothing he could do could make her arrive any sooner, so he might as well wear it.

He sat like that for perhaps ten minutes, then he heard heavy footsteps down the other end of the hallway, and a door being buzzed. He heard some voices, then the footsteps came close, another door was buzzed, and he heard more voices. Then he heard the door close, and the footsteps came nearer to him, and his door was buzzed. He didn't like the sound of that. He went to the door and said loudly through it

"Who is it?"

"Police" came the answer. For a second panic leapt within him and he thought something had happened to Anna, but then he told himself, they would have come straight to his door, they wouldn't have been buzzing the other doors. Unless…they didn't know his unit number, just knew he lived in that block!

When he opened the door two young police officers were there, a young fresh-faced male and a young fresh-faced female.

"Sorry to trouble you sir, but are you aware that there was a bag snatch right outside this block of flats half an hour ago?" said the male policeman.

His first thought was thankfulness it was nothing to do with Anna. His second thought was that it was par for the course for this area. His third thought was that, supposing Anna had been walking in just at that time and it had been her who was the victim? Why, if anyone touched her he'd ram their head into a brick wall and then kick them until there was nothing left of them. His fourth thought was that – what a place he was inviting Anna to, bag snatchings right outside where he lived.

"No I didn't hear anything" he told them It was true, It had all happened a stone's throw from where he was and he had heard nothing.

"The elderly lady who was the victim thinks the assailant may have retreated into this building" said the female officer."The only description we have is that he might have been wearing a red jumper. Can you think of anyone in the building who might have been involved?'

Ron wished he could involve the little runt who had "borrowed" the five dollars from him. If only he could get him locked up! But he knew it wasn't him, it was too obvious, and he was too smart. Why would he snatch old womens' handbags when he had such a good racket going to make money other ways? He gave them a description of him, and his name and flat number, but the officers (not that Ron was surprised) already had had his name mentioned by two other tenants, and said they had interviewed him and he had an alibi.

The officers asked him to contact the local station if he had any information and then they left.

He closed the door thinking: that was all he needed! Now Anna would be arriving at a crime scene. The place was dirty enough, now it had been besmirched even more.

"What's been happening here, Dad?" she would ask.

"Oh only a bag snatch, and a few other things!"

He felt guilty at having to invite her to such a place. He should have been living in a stately home, with a manicured garden, and a long winding gravel drive that cars made a noise on when they drove up it. That was the only thing that would really be good enough for Anna.

That drove him into a kind of depressing self-examination of why he wasn't in a stately home with a manicured garden and long winding drive, and how he had ended up where he was today.

Then the phone rang. It was Anna.

"Dad".

Her voice was spiritless and timid and almost as if she was calling from the other side of the world on a bad line.

"I can't come"

She got the news out straightaway without beating round the bush, as was her way, but there was a mountain of apprehension and disappointment and guilt and everything else in the way she said it.

All he could do was let out a sort of primitive sound that was a cross between a wail and a groan.

He had tried in all the previous calls to sound like he understood and not get flustered, even though that was not the way he felt, but this time he could help losing it partially and squealing "But I was really looking forward to it, Anna, I've got everything prepared....I was so hoping you could make it!"

She suddenly became very voluble, and the words gushed out of her.

"I know, Dad, I'm really, really sorry. I really am. I really want to come over. You don't know how I feel having to make this call. But I just can't make it. I've just had a call from the States and I've got to re-do everything. I probably won't get any sleep before I get the plane tomorrow. I'll be lucky if I leave the office by dawn. I'll have to go straight home, pick my things up, change, and then leave straightaway for the airport. I'm sorry, Dad, I'm really sorry. I'm really, really sorry. I'll ring you as soon as I get to New York."

He could feel his anger getting the better of him. He knew if he spoke words they would be bad ones he would regret later, so all he allowed out of his lips was "Well…well….you know…."

She knew there was no more to be said so she just said "Bye, Dad. I'll call you from New York."

He put the receiver down gently, he couldn't slam it down, because she might have heard. but as soon as it was down, he stood stock still for a few seconds fuming, his rage against the world rising rapidly, then he kicked the chair that was near him so hard it flew over the other side of the room. Then he picked up a saucepan and threw that at the wall, Then he knocked a whole stack of jars and bottles and cups off the kitchen dresser with one backward movement of his arm. Then he picked up another chair and threw it. He had a motion to pull the whole white tablecloth off the set table and send all the crockery flying, but he just restrained himself. It was his old temper that had contributed to the wrecking of his marriage coming out again. He clenched his fists and raised then to each side of his head, and looked towards the ceiling and let out a wailing noise and walked round the flat like that for some minutes, wailing and kicking everything that got in his way. He was finding it hard to fight back tears. Then he slumped in a chair at the table and put his head in his hands over the perfect white table cloth and the glistening china and silver ware as if he was suddenly aware of the futility of all that. Then the idea came into his mind that he would never see her again. It was an omen, she would stay overseas for ever now.

Life wasn't worth living if he didn't have Anna. He was still wailing - a primitive, chilling, inhuman sound. Then, suddenly, he jumped up and went to a cupboard and took out a bottle of port. He tore the top off and started guzzling it down. In two minutes he had swallowed a quarter of the bottle, He went over to his favourite armchair, not the table this time, and sat down, and started drinking some more.

He could see all those pictures of Anna on the walls, he was so glad they were only pictures and not really her to see him. In half an hour, he knew they would all disappear into a blurry haze.

He drank some more. And, oh, it tasted good! It tasted so good!